The Chalet School

D0608678

FREE GIFTS FROM
THE ARMADA COLLECTORS' CLUB

Look out for these tokens in your favourite Armada series! All you need to do to receive a special FREE GIFT is collect 6 tokens in the same series and send them off to the address below with a postcard marked with your name and address including postcode. Start collecting today!

Send your tokens to:

Armada Collectors' Club
HarperCollins Children's Books,
77 - 85 Fulham Palace Road,
London, W6 8JB

Or if you live in New Zealand to:

Armada Collectors' Club
HarperCollins Publishers Ltd.
31 View Road,   Glenfield,
PO Box 1,   Auckland

THIS OFFER APPLIES TO RESIDENTS OF THE U.K., EIRE AND NEW ZEALAND ONLY.

1 TOKEN

CS

The Chalet School series by Elinor M. Brent-Dyer

The Head Girl of the Chalet School

Elinor M. Brent-Dyer

Armada
An Imprint of HarperCollinsPublishers

First published in 1928 by Chambers Ltd
First published inpaperback in 1970 by
William Colllins Sons & Co. Ltd.
This impression 1992

Armada is an imprint of HarperCollins Children's Books,
a division of HarperCollins Publishers Ltd,
77–85 Fulham Palace Road, Hammersmith,
London W6 8JB

Printed and bound in Great Britain by
HarperCollins Book Manufacturing Ltd, Glasgow.

Contents

CHAPTER 1

The Coming Term

Two girls were walking down Palmerston Road, Portsmouth, with a graceful swing which drew the eyes of the passers-by to them. The elder of the two, slender and pretty, with an unusual amount of brown curling hair tied loosely back from a vivid face, was holding forth to the other, a smaller girl, with black eyes shining out of a pale pointed face, which looked the paler for the straight black hair cut round it, in page boy fashion.

"It's going to be difficult, you see, Joey," said the older girl as they paused before a café, where they evidently expected to meet someone. "If only Madame hadn't gone and got married this year!" she added.

Joey pulled her brown hat more firmly on to her head before she replied. "I think you are a bit selfish about that, Grizel," she said mildly. "After all, she did wait a whole year before she did it, and it's worse for Robin and me than for you."

"I do wish Bette had stayed on till the end of the year," said Grizel. "After all, she's only just eighteen, and heaps of girls go to school long after that. Why, the Head of the High was nearly nineteen!"

"Yes; and now she's at Oxford," said Joey. "Bette is only going to be at home. I'm sorry if you feel like that about it, but it can't be helped! — And there's Maynie and the Robin *at last*!"

The two girls turned to look down the road to where a tall, graceful girl of twenty-two or three was coming along, holding the hand of a small girl of eight, whose lovely little face was lifted to her companion's as she talked rapidly and eagerly, with gesticulations which, in Robin Humphries, were not surprising, as she was half Polish.

As they saw the two girls awaiting them, the pair hurried

7

their steps, and presently they were all seated round a table, chattering away, while Miss Maynard, who was maths mistress at the Chalet School to which they belonged, gave her orders to the waitress.

"Didn't know you were coming, Robin," said Joey, as she helped the small girl to unfasten her coat and hang up her hat. "Thought you were going to stay with Mrs Maynard this morning."

"It was such a fine day," said the mistress, "that I thought she might as well come. She loves Portsmouth — don't you, *mein Vöglein*? And we go back tomorrow."

"Isn't it joyous?" said Joey eagerly. "I love England, of course; but the Tyrol is home now, and I'm dying to see my sister again! How she *could* be so stupid as to get mumps at Christmas is more than I can think! It's messed up her holidays, anyway!"

"Poor Tante Marguérite!" said the Robin pensively. "Will she be quite well now, Joey? Shall we go to see her when we get home?"

"Sure of it," said Joey. "Shouldn't wonder if she wasn't at Innsbruck waiting to welcome us."

"I wish Madame was back at the chalet!" sighed Grizel, her mind reverting to her own particular problems once more. "It won't be easy this term — Easter term never is!"

"But you've been games prefect long enough to be able to carry responsibility," said Miss Maynard bracingly. "Why are you so upset about being head girl?"

"Games give you a certain hold," explained Grizel. "Gertrud will do well as games prefect, she'd have done just as well as head girl. I wish I hadn't been chosen. Of course, I shall do my best, Miss Maynard; but it *won't* be easy."

"Nothing worth while ever is," replied the mistress. Then she changed the conversation. It was true that the Robin never repeated things; still, it was better that she should not hear Grizel's woes voiced quite as plainly as this. Therefore Miss Maynard turned to Joey and asked her some question about the books she had come to buy.

"Got three of them," replied the girl. "The Francis Thompson was five bob, but worth it! The Green's history was five too. The other thing was sixpence."

"I can't understand *how* you can read those awful goody-good books," interposed Grizel. "It isn't you a bit, really!"

"I think they're so priceless," said Joey, with a grin. "And, anyway, they do teach you a lot of history."

"But they're so biased," objected Grizel. "The one you lent me seemed to be fairly reeking with hate for the English and George III and his ministers. It's so silly, too, when it all happened more than a hundred years ago."

"Well, they had a lot to put up with," said Joey broad-mindedly. "After all, Grenville and his idiotic Stamp Act was enough to drive anyone mad, especially when they hadn't a chance of saying anything one way or another. And Miss Annersley says that it was a very good thing for us that the American colonies *did* break away. So it was all for the best."

Grizel shrugged her shoulders. She was not historically inclined, and, to her way of thinking, it didn't really matter whether the Americans had remained part of the empire, or whether they broke away from it. She simply could not understand Joey Bettany's interest in people long since dead and gone. They finished their lunch with an amiable dis-cussion of books for the school library, in which even the Robin joined, for she read a good deal for her eight years, and had her own views on the subject of stories.

"We've got plenty to take with us," said Miss Maynard at last. "That case will be full now; and I won't have any more to look after than I can help. Your three must go in your suitcase, Jo. As it is, we shall have a good deal of luggage."

"That's the only bother about bringing books from England," said Grizel. "I've got one to put in *my* case too."

"Well, we can't help it," said Jo philosophically. "After all, we can't expect to get books there in English — at least, not all the books we want. — Yes, thank you, Miss Maynard, I've quite finished. Shall we get ready to go now?"

"Yes, I think so. Fasten up your coat collars, and collect your possessions, girls. — Jo, see to the Robin. — I want to go to the china shop to get one or two things, so we must hurry, as we ought to catch the early train if we possibly can. I don't like motoring through the forest after dark in this weather."

Miss Maynard made all the haste she could, and an hour later saw them in the train for Southampton, the girls glancing at their books while the mistress made up her accounts and the Robin peered out at the fast falling dusk. "Me, I do not like the English winter," she announced suddenly.

"Don't you, darling?" asked Miss Maynard absently, as she tried to balance her account. "Never mind; we'll soon be back at the Tiern See. You like winter there. Girls, we are nearly at Southampton; close your books and pack up, or we may miss the train. We shall have a rush as it is."

They got ready once more, and in the scurry for the little local train that took them to Lyndhurst, they forgot what they had been talking about. Once in the Lyndhurst train, they began discussing school once more, for all of them loved their school in the lovely, picturesque Tyrol.

It had been run by Joey Bettany's sister, Madge, until the previous summer, when she had married Dr James Russell, head of the big new sanatorium on an alp high up the Sonnenscheinspitze, a mountain on the opposite side of the lake. The present head was Mademoiselle Lapâttre, who had been joint head with Miss Bettany until her marriage. Miss Maynard was senior and mathematical mistress, and four other English girls formed the rest of the resident staff. An excellent matron ran the domestic side of the school, and Herr Anserl from Spärtz, the little market town at the foot of the mountains where the Tiern See lies, three thousand feet above sea level, came twice a week to give piano lessons to the most promising of the girls. Singing was taught by Mr Denny, who was obliged for the sake of his health to remain in the district, and whom the girls privately thought rather mad. Masters came from Innsbruck for the violin, cello, and harp; and young Mrs Russell had, for the last term, come down from the Sonnalpe twice a week to give lessons in English literature. This term, however, the state of the roads would make such a thing an impossibility. When March should come, bringing with it the rapid thaw, the paths would be well-nigh impassable on the lake side of the mountain, and Dr Jem, as all the girls called him, had vetoed the idea for that term, at any rate. Consequently, when Miss Maynard had informed her ex-head that she intended to spend the Christmas holidays at home, and had begged leave to take Joey and the Robin with her that they might have a really English Christmas, Mrs Russell had agreed. It suited her better, for her husband had been summoned to a medical conference at Vienna for the week between Christmas and New Year, and she naturally wanted to go with him. So Joey and Robin had come to England, and Grizel Cochrane had come with them to spend her Christmas at her own home in Devonshire. A week ago she had joined the others in the New Forest, and was to travel back with them to Austria. This would be her last year at the Chalet School, for she would be eighteen in May, and then she was to go to Florence to study music in earnest under one of the best masters there.

It cannot be said that Grizel looked forward to her future with much enjoyment. She was not really musical, though hours of practice rigorously enforced by her stepmother while she had been in England, and then carried on under Herr Anserl in Briesau, had made her a brilliant instrumentalist. What was to happen after Florence no one seemed to know. Grizel and her stepmother were not in sympathy with each other, and her father was too much immersed in his profession — he was a barrister with a wide practice — to care overmuch about the daughter he had seen comparatively rarely. Since she was ten, Grizel had been very much a lonely child, and to her the Chalet School was the only real home she had ever known.

It was home to Joey Bettany too, though she knew that her sister and brother-in-law wanted her to feel that the pretty

11

chalet outside the Sonnalpe stood for that now. She liked Jem very well, and she adored her sister, but Briesau, where she knew everyone and everyone knew her, was far dearer to her than the Sonnalpe with the big sanatorium and its sad community of people who had come there in search of health.

As for the Robin, she had been left motherless two years previously, and had been sent to the school while her father was in Russia on business. The business had long since been finished, and Captain Humphries was secretary to Dr Jem. The little girl was a frail creature, so, since she was happy at school, it was deemed better to keep her there, away from the sorrow of the Sonnalpe, except at holiday times, when she and Joey would generally be at the chalet, where her father lived with the doctor, "Uncle Jem", and his pretty wife.

So for all the girls, and also for Miss Maynard, whose eldest brother was assistant at the Sonnalpe, Briesau and the Chalet School meant far more than school ordinarily does. They had all enjoyed their stay in England, but they were all very glad to be returning to Austria, and they talked about it as they trundled along to Lyndhurst, where the Maynards' car would meet them, and whirl them through the forest for seven miles to Pretty Maids, the Maynards' big house.

"What I think is so wonderful," said Jo, as she accepted a lump of toffee from the sticky packet Grizel was offering her, "is the idea of seeing Basle. We've only rushed through in the train before, and I *do* like seeing new places. It's got heaps of history, too. All sorts of jolly interesting things happened there, and I'm simply yearning to see it!"

"You and history!" jeered Grizel, who was mathematically inclined, and regarded her history lessons as evils to be avoided.

"It's so jolly interesting! I like to know what people did and how they lived, and so on. It's heaps better than horrid old geometry and algebra, anyway!" retorted Joey, whose views on mathematics were revolutionary in the extreme.

At this point Miss Maynard thought it best to interfere.

Jo and Grizel were ordinarily good friends, but both had fiery tempers, and neither fully understood the other, so that battles between them were apt to be fierce if short-lived.

"There is plenty to see in Basle," she said. "I know Robin will love the Zoo — won't you, baby? And there is a very interesting museum and a good picture gallery."

"Wonderful!" approved Jo. "I love animals, and pictures are awfully interesting. What's in the museum, Maynie?"

Out of term, the girls were allowed to use this nickname of a popular mistress since they had stayed at her home more than once, and were very welcome visitors there.

"A good part of it is devoted to natural history," said Miss Maynard.

"Butterflies and things?" said Grizel.

"I suppose so. Then there is the picture gallery with some very famous pictures — one or two by Hans Holbein the Younger, I believe. There is a special history museum in the Barfüsser Kirche, which is famous. You will like the armoury collection and the treasury, I know, even if the historical side of them doesn't interest you. And you will want to see Father Rhine, of course."

"I love the Rhine, ever since I read *The First Violin*," agreed Grizel. "Of course, I'd rather see it at Cologne with the Bridge of Boats. Shall we have time to go to Schaffhausen to see the Falls?"

Miss Maynard shook her head. "I'm afraid not, Grizel. We are spending one day in Paris, and three in Basle, and Schaffhausen is a good four hours or so from Basle. You'll have to wait for that till the summer. Then, if we do as we have planned, I will take you there for a few days on our way to Cologne and the Rhine cities."

"But Joey and Robin won't be with us," objected Grizel. "I know it's awfully decent of you to say you'll take me to the Rhine cities before I go to Florence, but Jo is going to spend the summer hols with Elisaveta in Belsornia, and the Robin is to go to Paris with the Lecoutiers. Even Juliet won't be there, as she is going to the Sonnalpe to be with

13

Madame.'' She referred to Mrs Russell's ward, Juliet Carrick, who was at present at London University, reading for a mathematical degree.

"I'm sorry, Grizel," said Miss Maynard. "If we could do it, I should say 'yes' at once. But there will be a good deal to get through before term begins, and we shall have none too much time as it is. Later on we may be able to arrange for the four of you to go together."

Grizel gave up worrying, and as they were nearing Lyndhurst, they all gathered up their parcels and prepared to leave the train. But she had by no means given up the idea as yet. That was not Grizel Cochrane's way. It had led to trouble in the past, and was to do so again before she learned her lesson.

CHAPTER 2

Basle

"Now, have we got everything? Four cases — two bundles of rugs — your attaché cases — Grizel's music case — the picnic basket? Is that all? Then come along, girls, or we shall miss the train, and I don't want to do *that*! Come, Robin. Keep close to me."

Followed closely by the Robin and at a little distance by Grizel, Joey and a burdened porter, Miss Maynard walked down the long platform of the Gare de l'Est, where the Paris-Wien express was standing, and quickly found the carriage reserved for them. It was nearly nine at night, and they would reach Basle round about five the next morning; but all four were accustomed travellers, and Miss Maynard much preferred to do the travelling at night when the girls would be sleeping, than through the day, when active Grizel and Robin would find the time pass slowly. Joey was less of a trial on long train journeys, for she was always happy as long as she had a book.

The mistress quickly made a nest for the Robin in one corner with rugs and an air-pillow, pulled off the sturdy little boots, and tucked her up comfortably. Tired from a long day in Paris, she fell asleep almost at once, heedless of the bright lights, the hoarse shouts of the busy porters. Miss Maynard then turned her attention to the girls.

Since they had been in Paris all day, and had been talking French, which came as naturally to them as their own tongue — all four were trilingual as a result of being in a school where English, French and German were all spoken freely — she fell into French in bidding them prepare for the night.

Joey and Grizel did as they were told to the extent of rolling themselves in rugs, and curling up on the seats which had been widened by pulling out a kind of under-seat. Experienced travellers, they slipped off their boots, exchanged their brown velour hats for tams, and in ten minutes were ready. The mistress herself did not attempt her preparations yet. She knew that she would read for an hour or two as soon as they got off. The children were different, and all were accustomed to early hours.

Then silence settled down over them all, and Miss Maynard presently fell asleep till a quarter to five when an attendant came along announcing that they were nearly into Basle, and would arrive there in ten minutes' time. Moving as quietly as she could, Miss Maynard woke up Joey and Grizel, and bade them get ready to leave the train. The Robin she left. The elder girls quickly and deftly put their things together, rolling up rugs, and strapping them with neatness and precision.

At this point the train slackened speed, and ran into the deserted station, where only the flaring lights and a few sleep-eyed porters spoke of the life that thronged it through the day. Miss Maynard leaned out of the window, and summoned one to come and get their things, while she herself picked up the Robin, who slept on serenely through it all, and Joey and Grizel took their rugs.

Soon they were on their way to their pension, where a drowsy night-porter let them in. They all went straight to bed, and slept till noon.

*   *   *

Joey was the first to wake up. She sat up in bed, wide awake in a moment. Then she looked across to where Grizel lay, still fast asleep in the bed in the corner.

She looked very pretty as she lay there, her cheeks rose-flushed with sleep, and her long brown curls scattered over the pillow. But aesthetic sights were not in Miss Bettany's mind at the moment. Moving quietly, she lifted her pillow, stood up in bed to get a surer aim, and then hurled it well on to Grizel's face.

That young lady sat up with a muffled howl, wildly clearing

16

curls and sleep-mists out of her eyes while the pillow fell to the floor. "Joey Bettany! You little brute! And I was having such a gorgeous dream!"

"Time you were beyond dreams, my dear!" retorted Joey, curling herself up on the bed, and hauling the *plumeau* round her shoulders. "It's midday! Nearly time for *Mittagessen*! Get up, you lazy object!"

"Lazy object yourself!" said Grizel indignantly. "You've only just wakened yourself! I know you, Jo Bettany! And if you hurl any more things at me I'll yell the house down. I say! there's someone coming — chambermaid or something! Cave!"

Joey made a wild dive, and when the round-cheeked Gretchen came in bearing rolls and honey and coffee on a tray for the two, she found them both lying very properly in bed, though the younger fräulein did not seem to have any pillow, and the other one had two!

When she had gone, Joey sat up, and demanded her pillow back again.

"No fear!" retorted Grizel. "You chucked it at me most brutally, so now you may do without! It's no good coming and scrapping for it, for you'll only upset the coffee if you do, and then there'll be a row! Stop it, Joey! You'll have the tray all over the bed if you go on like this!"

"Give me my pillow, then!" retorted Jo, hauling away at it with such goodwill that she finally succeeded in getting it out from under Grizel's shoulders, nearly upsetting the tray and its contents as she did so. With a cry of triumph she darted back to her own bed and *Frühstück*.

"Pig!" said Grizel indignantly. "You *are* a little horror, Joey!"

"Hurry up and get on," was the only answer Joey vouch-safed as she devoured her rolls and honey, and drank the bowl of milky coffee which she appreciated far more than the tea she had in England.

Seeing nothing else to do, Grizel did as Joey suggested, and presently they were dressed in their pretty frocks, so that when Miss Maynard came, as she imagined, to waken them, they were standing at the window, looking out at the quiet street below, ready dressed. They turned as she entered.

"*Grüss Got*," said Joey, with the charming Tyrolean greetings which she loved so. "Oh, Maynie! Just look at those darling dogs!"

Miss Maynard laughed as she crossed the room, and looked out of the window at the sight she had expected to see — a low-wheeled cart with big milk-can slung across it, and drawn by two big dogs, who were padding sedately along as if they knew how important was their charge. The whole equipage was guarded by a small boy of about ten, who bore a long whip, which he cracked continually to encourage his steeds, not that they took any notice of either it or him.

"Jo! You baby!" laughed Miss Maynard. "You must have seen the same thing dozens of times before this! They do it in practically every European country! I'm sure you saw it when you were in Munich!"

"Yes; I know," agreed Joey. "But those are such *dear* dogs — nearly as nice as my Rufus!"

"They aren't the same breed," said Grizel critically. "Rufus is a St Bernard, and I don't know what you would call those!"

"Just plain dog, I should think," said Miss Maynard as she turned from the window. "Well, I came to call you two; but as you are ready, I will go back to Robin. *Mitagessen* is at one, but I didn't think we should want any so soon after *Frühstück*. What do you say to going out now? We can get *Kaffee* at a *pâtisserie*, and you can make up for it at our evening meal. Do you agree?"

"Oh, rather!" cried Jo. "Where are we going first? I want to see that history museum you told us about. Can we go there?"

"If you like. I believe the Robin is longing for the Zoo. What would you like, Grizel?"

"I'd like to look at the shops and the town," said Grizel.

"Well, we can't do everything," said Miss Maynard, with

18

a little inward smile for the difference between the two girls shown in their replies to her question. "We might look at the shops, and also see the Barfüsser Kirche today, if you like. Then tomorrow we must give the Robin her turn, and go to the Zoo. In the afternoon I should like to see the museum in the Augustinergasse — that's where the picture gallery is, Grizel. Then on Thursday we might explore the town, and see some of the old university buildings. Basle is one of the oldest university towns in Europe, you know, and any number of famous men came here during the Renaissance. Does that programme meet with your approval?"

"Oh, yes," said Joey emphatically.

But Grizel shook her head. "I do so want to go to Schaffhausen and see the Falls. Couldn't we possibly?"

"No, Grizel," said Miss Maynard. "I've already said we can't. In any case, this is not the weather to go and see waterfalls. I have told you I will take you in the summer; please let that be sufficient."

"What on earth makes you so mad on the Rhine Falls, Grizel?" Joey asked curiously when Miss Maynard had gone off to help the Robin to dress. "You are an ass to fuss like this. Maynie won't go, and you ought to know it by this time. She always means what she says."

But Grizel was a determined young lady, and when she took an idea into her head it required a good deal of dislodging. She had by no means put Schaffhausen out of her thoughts, as Joey was to find later on. Now, she merely requested the younger girl not to bother her, and began to get into her hat and coat.

It was a cold day, colder than it had been in Portsmouth, but it was a dry, bracing cold, and as they were warmly wrapped up, they looked forward to their walk. At Briesau it had to be very bad weather for the girls to be kept indoors. So Joey and Grizel put on stout boots, and tied big scarves across their chests, and turned up the fur collars on their coats, and when they had wriggled into their warm woollen mitts, felt ready for anything. Miss Maynard and

19

the Robin, similarly attired, met them at their door, and they all trooped downstairs, laughing and chattering.

The first thing to do was to get to the shops, for Grizel was anxious to see them and to buy some ribbons to send to "Cooky" in her far-away Devonshire home. Cooky had always been a great ally of hers, and Grizel remembered many a kindness the big buxom woman had shown her, and always did her best to repay. Ribbon from Basle to trim her new spring hat would be greatly appreciated. It was a good point in a character that was inclined to be hard, and the Chalet School people had always encouraged it. The discipline Grizel had undergone at the hands of her step-mother for four and a half years had been very bad for the girl. As a consequence of it, she fought for her own hand first, and was very selfish, only trying to get what *she* wanted, without much regard for other people. It was, as Mrs Russell had said at the end of the previous term, when she was discussing the point with Mademoiselle, a big experiment putting Grizel into the position as head girl. "She will either do magnificently — or she will fail badly," she had said. "But, Elise, I feel sure that Grizel will try to make a success of it. It may make all the difference to her in after life. And we have only these two last terms to influence her. After that she goes to Florence, and it is out of our hands."

Mademoiselle had agreed, and so they had sent for Grizel, and had informed her of their decision. As has been seen, she had been disturbed by it. She knew, for Mrs Russell had told her, that to be successful she must set the school first; herself last. Grizel hated to do anything and fail; but she did not like the sound of that "School first; self last". It looked as if things would not be too comfortable. She had tried to get out of it; had pointed out that Gertrud Steinbrücke was her age, and as old a Chaletian as she was; that she was Captain of the Games, and had her music to work at. It had all been of no avail.

"I want you to take it, and to do your best with it, Grizel," Mrs Russell had said, holding the girl's grey eyes with her own steady gaze as she spoke. "Come, dear! You say you have been happy here. It isn't asking much to ask you to give us your best work for the last two terms you will spend with us. I know you will come back to see us, Grizel, but it's not the same."

And, drawn to it by the appeal in those deep brown eyes fronting her, Grizel had agreed. But she had made a proviso to herself. She would accept, and would do her level best. School should come first all the time, and self should have a poor chance, so far as she could manage it; *but* — she would have her own way during the holidays.

They went gaily down the street. It was a glorious day for a walk, sharp and crisp, with a snap of frost in the air and frozen snow on the pavements crunching under their tread. The Robin danced along, clinging to Joey's hand, while Grizel herself walked demurely by the side of Miss Maynard, chattering to her in German. She had been far slower than Jo to pick up languages, but they had come at last through ceaseless practice. As for Jo, English, French, or German, it was all one to her. She knew a certain amount of Italian too, and had a slender portion of Russian, a fact which had proved of great use to her during the summer term, and which had been the means of rescuing her friend, Elisaveta, Crown Princess of Belsornia, from the hands of her father's cousin, a half-mad man, who had tried to kidnap and hold her as a hostage against her father, now King of Belsornia, and her grandfather, who had been the reigning king at that time. Elisaveta was now Crown Princess, and too important a personage to finish her education in any school, so she had had to go back to governesses in Belsornia. But the friendship between her and Jo was not likely to die, even though they could not meet, and Joey got letters every week from "Your loving Veta".

As in Portsmouth, people turned to look at them. All four were so graceful, moving with a free, easy grace that had its roots in constant practice of the old English folk dances. Miss Maynard smiled as she noted how elderly men looked at the Robin with her almost angelic loveliness, and how they smiled to receive one of her fearless beams at them.

In the shops she still attracted attention, and while Grizel was debating whether Cooky would like vivid purple or lurid green for her hat, the assistants were murmuring among themselves about "*das Engelkind*". The marvel was that the child was not made conceited by all the petting she had received. It never seemed to affect her in the least.

When, finally, Grizel had fixed on a green ribbon, which was bright enough to please Cooky, and yet did not scream at one, they went out and visited the toy shops, where the baby bought two little wooden bears, one for Inga Eriksen, and the other for Amy Stevens, these two people being her greatest friends. "And Tante Marguérite," she pleaded. "I have two francs left. What can I buy for Tante Marguérite?"

It was while Miss Maynard was helping her to choose a little wooden chalet that Grizel drew Jo to one side and said, "Joey, are you game for a rag?"

"Of course; what is it?" demanded Jo.

"You know I want to go to Schaffhausen and see the Rhine there? Well, let's go tomorrow when Maynie takes the Robin to the Zoo. We don't want to see it — there's only chamois and bears and things like that. We'll leave a note saying where we've gone, and slip off about eight in the morning. Then we can go there and see the Falls, and get back in the afternoon. Like the idea?"

"I think you must be mad," said Jo, staring at her. "Quite mad! There'd be a fiendish row, and we'd jolly well deserve it after treating Maynie like that when she's been so decent stopping here for three days to let us see the place! I knew you went off the rails sometimes, but I never thought you did it to that extent! It's one of the rottenest things I've ever heard of!"

Grizel was furious. It was bad enough to have a mere kid like Jo Bettany say such things to her; but what hurt most was the look in Joey's eyes. There was scorn there, and disgust. There was also that which reminded the elder girl of the time when she had run away in a fit of rage to climb the Tiernjoch, a dangerous mountain, perilling both her own life and Joey's in the attempt. Jo had followed her to fetch her back, and the pair had been caught in a mist on the verge of a dangerous precipice, where they had had to wait until help came. Jo had not meant to remind the elder girl of this, but Grizel remembered all the same. It added to her fury, and she flung herself away with a low "Little *prig*!" which brought the angry colour to Jo's face. Happily, before anything further could happen, the Robin appealed to them for assistance in making up her mind which of the two chalet models she should choose, and by the time this knotty point was settled both looked more or less normal again. They were far enough from feeling it though.

From the shops they went to the Barfüsser Kirche, a church dating from the fourteenth century, but now used as the historical museum. There the Lallenkönig attracted the Robin, and she insisted on standing to watch the head stick out its tongue and roll its eyes at her. They could scarcely get her away. However, Miss Maynard finally got them to the great collection of arms, where Joey revelled to her heart's content in the curious weapons of the ages, weaving stories about them in her head, while Grizel wandered round, interested in the growth and development of warfare. From the armoury they went to the series of rooms intended to show the development in the furnishing and arranging of rooms from the fifteenth century onwards, and here Jo was in her element indeed. She invented stories for the Robin about the people who had lived in the different rooms, and gave them the most astonishing adventures. The Robin was entranced. Miss Maynard had to cut them short, or they would never have seen the rest of the building.

The Treasury, containing relics of the days when Basle had been one of the foremost of the Catholic sees, didn't interest them half so much, though Joey looked at the beautiful altar vessels with awe, and was specially pleased with the reminders of Erasmus, the great Renaissance scholar,

23

who became the friend of Sir Thomas More, one of her heroes. She was rather disappointed to find no relics of her favourite Napoleon, but the rooms containing the musical instruments, quaint old citherns and citoles, lutes and harps, and the beautiful specimens of stained glass delighted her.

"Only think," said Jo, pausing before one beautiful example of a cithern. "Laura may have played to Petrarca on that!"

"What on earth do you know about Laura and Petrarca?" demanded Miss Maynard in astonishment.

"Oh, only that they were lovers, and he wrote sonnets to her, and invented a type of sonnet," returned Jo.

After that Miss Maynard decreed that it was time for *Kaffee*, and hustled them all out and to a *pâtisserie*, where they had milky coffee and delicious cakes, all honey and nuts and cream. If Grizel was a little quiet, no one noticed it, and the other two made up for her silence. They had to hurry back to the pension in the end, for it was getting late, and *Abendessen* was at seven. The Robin had rolls and butter and milk in bed, but the others went down and made a good meal, after which they went out for a walk along the lighted streets, where sleighs were dashing along the snowy roads, and the night was gay with the jangling of sleigh bells.

When they came in it was after nine, so Miss Maynard declared that they should all go to bed. She saw the other two to their room, made sure they had everything they wanted, and then left them, bidding Grizel see that the light was switched off at ten.

As soon as she had done, Joey dropped the frock she had just taken off on to a chair, and turned to Grizel. "Now," she said.

CHAPTER 3

The Falls of Rhine

Grizel turned sharply at the word, and looked at the other girl. "What do you mean?" she asked coldly.

"I'm going to have it out with you — that's all!" Joey sat down on the edge of her bed and looked Grizel squarely in the face.

"Have what out? And I do wish, Jo, you would try to remember, occasionally, that I am nearly three years older than you are. You speak sometimes as if you thought I were as old as — as — the Robin."

"I don't think you're as old, sometimes," retorted Joey. "You don't behave like it."

"That will do! Even if we do go away together for holidays, that's no reason why you should cheek me like this. I'm head girl, remember!"

"I wish *you* would try to remember it!" said Joey fervently. Then her tone changed. "Grizel, don't go to Schaffhausen! It isn't playing the game by Maynie! If you want us with you, I'll ask if I can go in the summer before I go to Belsornia to Elisaveta." But her first words had done the mischief, and even this sacrifice had no effect on Grizel, who could be thoroughly wrong-headed on occasion. She now looked at the younger girl with an expression of scorn, and said, "Mind your own business!"

"But, Grizel—" began Jo.

"That will do! I'm not going to be spoken to like that by a mere Middle. If you can't talk about anything else, you'd better be silent. Anyway, I don't want to talk to you. You're a bit swollen-headed, Jo. I suppose it's because Madame is your sister. It's a pity, because you *could* be quite a nice child, if it weren't for that."

Jo went white with anger at this unpleasant speech, but she said nothing. She got up from her bed, and went on with her undressing. Grizel followed her example, and they went to bed in utter silence. Joey had a hot temper, and Grizel had said an unforgivable thing just now. Things were at a deadlock.

Grizel soon fell asleep, for she was not imaginative, and, angry as she was, her emotions were little likely to disturb her rest. Joey, sensitive and temperamental, tossed about restlessly in her bed for two hours or more before she finally dropped off.

Grizel woke up at six o'clock in the morning, and, as soon as she was sufficiently wide awake to realize what had occurred the night before, slipped out of bed, and, with a cautious glance at the bed in the opposite corner, switched on the little reading lamp over her own. Then she dressed herself swiftly and warmly, putting on her thickest things. She had determined to get to the Falls of Rhine somehow, and knew that to do so she must make an early start. She wasn't sure how far Joey's sense of duty might carry her, either. That young lady scorned to tell tales, but no one knew better than Grizel that this was a case when she might rightfully feel that she was reporting, and not "sneaking".

Jo slept on soundly, and never stirred when the door opened and her companion slipped out and shut it carefully after her. She slept on till long after her usual time for waking, and, indeed, until Miss Maynard, wondering at the unusual quiet in their room, came along to see that they were all right.

In the meantime Grizel, her head held very high, ordered hot coffee and rolls for herself at the reception desk, and consumed them when they came in as airy a fashion as if she were not doing things she knew very well to be wrong. To the *Kellnerin* who served her she said that she was going on to Schaffhausen by the early train, and the others would join her later. She felt pretty safe in saying that last, for she knew that Miss Maynard, at any rate, would come to seek her and she had no intention of hiding from her once she had got her own way. She had made inquiries the night before, and had found that there was two hours between the

26

train by which she intended travelling and the next one. By that time, as she reckoned, she would have seen all she wanted to see, and would be quite content to come home. She finished her meal, and then set off for the Bahnhof.

Basle is a very old and picturesque city, and the long streets, with their quaintly gilded and frescoed houses, had reminders at every corner of the time when Basle was one of the great university towns of Europe. When Grizel reached the Badenischbahnhof, she found that she had just time to get her ticket for Schaffhausen.

It was still dusk, and mists lay low over everything. Grizel felt in her satchel for her book, and settled down for a good read. People passing the compartment in which she was seated looked curiously at her. In Switzerland a young girl of the upper classes no more roves about by herself than her sister in other European countries does. There is a great deal of freedom, it is true, but *la jeune fille* is well chaperoned for all that. To see a girl of seventeen quite without any relative or maid to look after her was unusual. When the daylight finally came, with bright wintry sunshine, Grizel put aside her book to look at the view, without any idea that she had aroused such interest.

She found the landscape uninspiring on this cold morning, when everything was covered with snow, and there were no mountains such as she loved. The railway here runs through the Rhine valley, which is low-lying, and only shows gentle undulations till it nears the environs of Zurich. It is a fairly populous valley, but Grizel was bored with the towns — and she soon lost interest in them and returned to her book. But this, too, seemed to have become dull, and so she took refuge in her thoughts. She wondered what they were saying at Basle. She could imagine Joey's indignation when she woke up and found herself alone. Miss Maynard would be furious, of course, and the Robin would be full of wonder. It wouldn't be a pleasant journey back to Innsbruck.

For the first time, Grizel began to repent her daring. After all, her idea at first had been to have Joey with her, and here she was — alone. If Jo hadn't been so emphatic, she would have left it alone. Then she pulled herself up short. It wasn't playing the game to blame Joey — Grizel rather prided herself on being fair. It was rather unfortunate that she had got on to that tack, for now a doubt came into her mind as to whether she was playing fair anyhow. Miss Maynard would be worried, she knew, and, after all, she *was* head girl. Suddenly she sat bolt upright. An awful thought had struck her. What if Madame, who still had a good deal to do with the school, should think that, since she had gone off in this mad way, she wasn't fit to be head girl?

Grizel's eyes widened in horror at the idea. If it were so, she could never stay on at the school. Everyone knew that she had been chosen, and the disgrace of being degraded would be more than she could endure.

The slowing down of the train warned her at this point that they were nearing a station. She would get out and go back at once. With Grizel, to think was to act. She collected her things in double quick time, and when they drew up by the platform at Waldshut, went along the corridor, and descended the little steps, and made for the barrier. There she had no easy time of it in explaining to the ticket collector why she had got out at a place twenty-four miles before the destination marked on her ticket. At first he thought that she had made a mistake, and got out, thinking she was already at Schaffhausen. Her bungling explanation that she had forgotten something — so she had! — roused deep suspicion in his mind. However, he could see nothing for it but to let her go, and told her when the next train back to Basle was. She found she had forty minutes' wait before her, and the snow had begun to fall again. She decided to go out and find a *pâtisserie*, and see if she could get chocolate and cakes. She went out into the street, feeling rather forlorn, and, after losing herself twice, managed to find a shop. She had spent so long over finding it that she had to hurry, and scalded her mouth with the hot chocolate.

Then it was helter-skelter back to the station, where she only just caught her train, and had to find a seat in a crowded compartment with two or three voluble Swiss ladies who talked the whole time, an old curé, who read his breviary industriously, and two youths of school age who were obviously Germán, and who stared at her unceasingly, and made remarks about her and giggled to each other. Of all the uncomfortable journeys she had ever taken, that struck Grizel as the worst. It seemed a never-ending age before she saw that they were nearing Basle, and then she could have cried with relief. As soon as the train drew up inside the station she was out of it and off through the streets, where the snow was now whirling down, as hard as she could go. At length she turned into the Sternen Gasse, where their pension was, and made her best pace along it. The doors were shut, of course, and she had to wait while the porter came to open them. When he saw her he exclaimed in surprise, but Grizel was past minding that. She pushed past him and along to the stairs, where she was met by the manageress, who was coming down. At sight of the English girl she stopped with uplifted hands. "Fräulein Cochrane! But *das Fräulein* has gone to seek thee at Schaffhausen!"

"Well, I'm here," said Grizel. "Where are the other two?"

Frau Betts looked at her severely. "Fräulein Bettany and *das Liebling* have gone too. Fräulein Maynard said that they would go straight to Innsbruck from Schaffhausen once they had found you. They have taken the luggage — all of it. Fräulein Maynard was very angry — as in truth she had every right to be! She said she would not feel happy till she had you all safely with your relatives. They have been gone these two hours!"

Grizel sat down limply on the stairs. She had got herself into a nice mess! If she had had any sense she would have wired them from Waldshut, and then no one would have gone chasing off after her. As it was, she had no idea what to do or where to go.

She did the best thing she could have done for herself.

Worn out, remorseful, and hungry, she forgot her pride and burst into tears.

At the sight Frau Betts, who was a good-natured soul, forgot her indignation, and hastened to apply comfort. "Hush, *mein Kind*! You are wearied, and must rest. Fritzi shall hasten to the post office and send a telegram to the station at Schaffhausen to say that you are here. You shall have a meal, and we will send you to them there. Come to my room."

She led the tearful girl to her own little sitting room, and made her lie down on a sofa. Then she came with a tempting little meal on a tray, and after the girl had eaten all she could, sent the long-suffering Fritzi out once more to seek a *droschke.* Into this she packed Grizel, seeing that she was warm and comfortable. Then she bade her *Auf Wiedersehen* and went back into the pension, shutting the door firmly behind her.

Oh, that weary journey! Grizel couldn't fix her mind on her book, for she was too worried over what Frau Betts had said about Miss Maynard's anger. She positively shivered when she learned that they were nearing Neuhausen, the station for the Falls, and for a moment she felt as if she would have preferred to stay where she was. However, cowardice was not one of Grizel's faults, so she pulled herself together and left the train as bravely as she could. At the other side of the barrier she saw Miss Maynard waiting for her — a very grave Miss Maynard, who made no comments, good, bad, or indifferent, on her behaviour, but simply bade her hurry up and get into the sleigh that she had hired.

Grizel did as she was told in dreary silence, and no word was spoken till they reached the hotel. There she was bidden to get out, and go in at once. In the vestibule she waited till Miss Maynard joined her and, still in that terrifying silence, led her to the room where Joey and the Robin awaited them.

At sight of Grizel the Robin ran forward, but Miss Maynard stopped her.

"No, Robin; not yet. Take off your things, Grizel.

Put them on that sofa for the time being. Now I want an explanation of your conduct."

Grizel stood there, twisting her fingers together. 'I — I'm very sorry,'' she said.

"I hope you are," said Miss Maynard, still in that grave, cold voice. "You have given us all, Frau Betts, Joey, and myself, a very anxious time. You have given us needless trouble, and added to our length of journey. If there is anything that will serve as an excuse for your conduct, I want to hear it."

Grizel stood there, fighting desperately with her tears.

Joey saw it, and braved the mistress's wrath. "Grizel," she said. "I honestly didn't mean to put your back up. If it was what I said made you do it, it's my fault as much as yours. I *am* a tactless ass!"

It was a way out; but Grizel had her code, and she stuck to it. "It was my own idiocy, Joey," she said.

"But I expect it was my being so beastly about it made you go on and do it," urged Joey, whose soft heart couldn't bear to see Grizel look so unhappy. "Word of honour, Miss Maynard, I'll bet it was me as much as anything! You know what I am!"

Miss Maynard looked at her. "Yes, Joey, I know. But Grizel—"

She got no further, for Grizel interrupted her. "It wasn't really Joey at all! I wanted to go, so I just — went. It's like that time I went off to climb the Tiernjoch. You'd think I'd have learnt a little sense from that, but I haven't! I'm awfully sorry, Miss Maynard. I simply didn't think. I know I'm not fit to be head girl now."

"Oh, tosh!" said Jo easily. "Of course you are. Maynie will forgive you 'cos you are sorry — won't you, Maynie?"

Miss Maynard shook her head. "It's not so easy as all that, Jo. As Grizel herself says, if she can go off like this for a mere whim, then she *isn't* fit to be Head at the Chalet School. We've got to feel we can depend on our head girl."

"Well, you will on Grizel after this," declared Joey.

"Anyhow, this isn't schooltime — it's hols! So do let it go at that, won't you? I'm sure Madge would."

"Do you think so?" asked Miss Maynard with a smile.

"Yes. She always trusts us to carry on and do our best. Look at the times she's forgiven *me* for doing mad things!"

"I shall have to tell her," said Miss Maynard, taking a sudden decision. "It will lie in her hands, Grizel. Meanwhile, we had better go and have *Kaffee*. Our train goes at six, and I want to see about one or two things. As far as I am concerned, the thing is shelved for the moment."

Luckily the Robin created a diversion by flinging herself on the girl. "*Pauv'* Grizel," she murmured.

Grizel picked her up and hugged her, thankful to hide her face among the black curls for a minute or two. When she looked up again Miss Maynard had gone off to see the manager about *Kaffee* and a picnic basket, for they would not get into Innsbruck till the next day. Nothing further was said, and they embarked on the last part of their journey very peacefully.

CHAPTER 4

Home Again

"Innsbruck at last! What ages it has seemed since the tunnel! Buck up, Robinette! We're nearly in! Pack up, Grizel. We're almost there! Oh, hurrah for dear little Innsbruck and Madge."

It was Joey, of course. The rest of the party got their things together in more orderly fashion, while she hung out of the window, talking and gesticulating wildly as the great train swept through the suburbs of Innsbruck, and finally slowed down by the platform. Standing waiting on it was a slight, graceful girl — she looked no more — clad in long green coat with big fur collar turned up, and a soft green hat. Her face was flushed with excitement, and as her dark eyes encountered the wildly waving Jo at the window they glowed with welcome. As the train stopped, Joey made a wild dive along the corridor and nearly fell down the steps into her sister's arms. "Madge — Madge! It's wonderful to see you again!"

"It's splendid to see you, Joey," replied the voice she loved better than any other sound in the world. "You've grown again, you monkey! You're as tall as I am now!" Madge Russell looked with a smile at the clever, sensitive face on a level with her own, and then turned to greet the others. "Robin! My little Cecilia Marya! Have you had a good time, *mein Vöglein*?"

The Robin, clasped tightly in the arms that had come to take the place of her mother's, tucked her curly head into "Tante Marguérite's" neck, and squeezed her rapturously. "Oh, so nice! Tante Marguérite, *bien aimée*, I do so *love* you!"

"Well, leave a little of me for the others, my pet!" laughed Mrs Russell as she set the little girl down and turned to greet Miss Maynard and Grizel.

The latter flushed under the welcoming kiss, but her ex-Head didn't notice it, for she was shaking hands with Miss Maynard, and asking questions as to their journey. "Did you have a good time, Mollie? Decent fellow-travellers? We just got back from Vienna two days ago. It was so jolly. We stayed with the von Eschenaus — they are back again. And I've got some news for you all. Wanda is betrothed."

"Who to?" demanded Joey as they all moved to the barrier.

"A young officer in her father's regiment."

"Gee! How priceless! Fancy Wanda engaged! That makes two of our old girls! First Gisela, and now Wanda! When's she to be married?"

"In the summer. I met him while we were there, and he is a charming young man. He adores Wanda, and she him, so I think they will be very happy." Madge Russell, happily married herself, smiled reminiscently. "You will hear all about it from Maria when term begins. She was wildly excited about it. Wanda is very sweet, and is longing for the spring to come. They mean to pay us a visit at Briesau then. She wants to show him her English school."

Joey sighed. "It's awfully nice for them, of course — I mean Gisela and Wanda. But it does seem as though we were all growing up frightfully quickly! Don't you think they are too young, Madge?"

"Gisela is twenty and Wanda is nineteen. And at least we shall have Gisela fairly near us. I am so glad Gottfried Mensch decided to join Jem at the Sonnalpe. I shall like to have my first head girl living next door, so to speak." She smiled at the new head girl as she spoke, but Grizel looked very grave. She was wondering whether she would be allowed to follow in the footsteps of Gisela Marani now. Luckily the Robin tugged at Mrs Russell at that moment, so the girl's expression passed without comment for the moment, though Madge Russell had noticed it, and wondered what it meant.

"Tante Guito" — the Robin sometimes abbreviated the longer name this way — "are we to stay with Onkel Riese and Tante Gretchen?"

Madge laughed at the "Uncle Giant", a name of Joey's bestowing on the kindly father of two of the Chalet School girls, who had been a great friend of theirs ever since the school had been opened. Then she nodded, "Yes, littlest and best! They would have come to meet us, but they thought I should like you to myself at first."

"Where's Jem?" asked Joey.

"He had to go back to the Sonnalpe at once," explained his wife as she tucked the Robin into the big sleigh which was awaiting them in the Bahnhof Platz, and which they had reached by this time. "He is looking forward to seeing you all tomorrow. You are to come to us for the rest of the week, you know."

"Good!" Joey heaved a rapturous sigh, and then sank down into her corner on the other side of her sister.

"Has Mademoiselle come back yet?" asked Miss Maynard as she took her seat facing them, with Grizel by her side.

"Yes; she arrived yesterday. Simone is with her, but Renée has a sprained ankle, so Madame Lecoutier is keeping her at home till half term. Then she will bring her, and see the school for herself. Cosy, Robin?"

"Yes, thank you," replied the Robin, slipping her hand into the slender one at her side. "Tante Marguérite, have Gisela and Gottfried arranged for their wedding yet?"

"Yes; that's another piece of news for you. But Gisela was to be at Maria Hilfe, so I am going to leave her to tell you all about it. She wants you three to be her bridesmaids, with Frieda and Maria, I know. Wanda is to be married in August too."

"Shall we go to Wien for that?" asked Joey anxiously. "I hope it won't be late, or it will cut up my time with Elisaveta. Have you any idea of the date, Madge?"

"It will be during the first week," said Mrs Russell. "As for cutting up your visit to Belsornia, Elisaveta will be there too, and I expect you will go back with her. At least the King said so wh'n he wrote to tell me about it."

"That's good; I suppose Wanda will have a very swish

wedding. Where will Gisela be married, do you think? In the Hof-Kirche?''

Madge refused to commit herself.

By this time they were driving down the Friedrich-Hertzog Strasse, making for the bridge, for the Maria Hilfe is a suburb across the river. Joey looked out at the busy streets, where sleighs were going about crunching the crisp snow under their shining runners and filling the air with the silvery jangle of bells. The celebrations of Christmas and New Year were over, but the shops still had a gay appearance. The snow lay thick on the ground and the steep roofs, and gave what the English girls were wont to call a ''Christmas card'' air to the town. It was early afternoon, but some of the shop windows were already lighted up. They turned down the Markt-Platz, and in a few minutes they were going smoothly along by the side of the Inn, which lay still and black under its coating of ice. Across the fine stone bridge they turned, and then they drove up the long Mariahilf Strasse to the door, where two tall, pretty girls of twenty or thereabouts were standing, eagerly awaiting them.

''Here at last!'' exclaimed the taller and fairer of the two as the sleigh stopped, and Joey scrambled out to be seized and kissed warmly by both. ''And our little bird! How well thou art, *mein Blümchen*!''

The Robin, well accustomed to endearments, held up her face for a kiss before she ran into the house, and began to skip up the stairs. It was a long way up, for the Mensches' flat was on the third floor. At length she was there, and springing into the arms of a slight girl of fifteen. Frieda Mensch was much smaller than the rest of her family, typically German, with long flaxen plaits on her shoulders, blue eyes, and an apple-blossom skin. She was very pretty, though by no means as attractive looking as her elder sister. Bernhilda, with her corn-coloured hair in a coronal of plaits round her head, was charming enough to have stood for one of the princesses in *Grimm's Tales*. A door opened at Frieda's joyful exclamations, and Frau Mensch, very fat, very fair like her daughters, rolled out and caught the visitors in a close embrace. "But how we have missed you, my children! There seemed to be something lacking in our joy this Christmas. *Die Grossmutter* has wearied for your return; she is in the salon now. Come, my children, and greet her."

She led the way to the long narrow salon where a tiny old woman, Herr Mensch's mother, was sitting by the big white porcelain stove. Old Frau Mensch was only two years short of her century, and she was very frail, but her eyes still snapped vividly, and she made herself felt in the little household. Joey went up to her, curtseying first in the pretty, old-fashioned way the old dame liked, and then offering her hand. The Robin followed her example, but she was kissed and crooned over.

Then Frau Mensch the younger — Tante Gretchen, as the girls had learned to call her — swept them all off for the meal, which she was sure they needed after their journey.

Joey heaved a sigh of joy as she settled down to a bowl of soup and a big slice of rye bread. "English food's all very well," she said, "but I love what we have here. I used to get so bored with the white bread. I *love* this!" She took a large bite out of her slice, and beamed on them all.

"Joey, you needn't act so like a little pig," said her sister severely. "Even if you *are* glad to get back, I think you might have a little less to say about your food! Was she like this in England, Grizel?"

She purposely included the elder girl in the conversation. That there was something wrong with Grizel was patent to anyone. Now, as the girl shook her head, she bit her lips. What *could* be the matter? However, it was no time to ask questions now, so she turned to Miss Maynard with some idle remark about the journey.

"Quite simple," was the answer. "Paris was delightful, and we had a good time seeing the shops at Basle."

"I thought you meant to stay longer," said Mrs Russell. "Why did you leave it so soon?"

"It was pouring with snow," said Joey hastily. "You never

saw anything like it! If it's going to be bad weather, it's best to be at home, *I* think!''

Madge frowned. Then she decided to say nothing, though Jo's rudeness in bursting in like this on her conversation with Miss Maynard was both unusual in her and outrageous. As for Grizel, she had no more to say, but ate her soup and bread, and drank the coffee which Bernhilda set before her. When the meal was over, the girls went off together for a chat, and the Robin, who was sleepy, was tucked up on the sofa to take a nap. Frau Mensch had some household tasks to see to, so she went out, leaving the other two together after excusing herself. She had barely closed the door behind her when Madge Russell turned eagerly to the other. ''Mollie! What is the matter? What happened at Basle? I'm sure something did, or you would never have come off so suddenly. Why on earth did you go to Schaffhausen at this time of year? I got the shock of my life when I got your wire from there saying you were coming back at once. And what is wrong with Grizel?''

Miss Maynard frowned. ''It's difficult to tell you, my dear. Yes, Grizel has been as mad as usual. I thought she was cured of wanting to go off on expeditions of her own, but evidently she isn't. As for Schaffhausen, it was her doing we went there. She ran away to see the Falls of Rhine yesterday morning without saying anything about where she was going, though she and Joey had had a battle royal over it the night before. Jo seems to think that it was partly her fault that Grizel went off as she did. There may be some truth in it. It's quite possible she did say things that put Grizel's back up. At the same time, Grizel has no excuse for going off as she did. If it hadn't been for what Jo was able to tell me, I shouldn't have known where she had gone. Then, when she was half way there, the silly child seems to have repented, and turned back — without wiring to let us know that she was returning. The result was that I packed up and took the other two off to Schaffhausen to seek her, and was met on the platform by a wire from Frau Betts saying that Grizel was there, and asking what they were to do. I wired them to send her on by the next train. She was very penitent, I must say, and has behaved very well since then. But honestly, my dear, I think we shall have to reconsider making her head girl. It seems to be impossible to place the smallest reliance on her."

Madge sighed. "Poor child! That's what's wrong with her, of course. She's dreading being degraded. I can't decide yet, Mollie; it's altogether too big a thing. And it's quite true that Jo can be horribly tactless when she is roused. I wish I knew what to do!" She got up, and began to pace backwards and forwards.

Miss Maynard watched her. She saw the difficulties, but she was not blessed with much imagination, and she did not know Grizel as well as the ex-Head did. To her way of thinking, it would be very unwise to risk having such a girl as head girl of the school. "It's hard luck on Grizel," she agreed; "but what else are you to do?"

"I can try her again," said Mrs Russell.

"My dear, how often have we done that already? Grizel has always been a problem."

"The trouble with Grizel is that she had far too much authority over her for four years. The second Mrs Cochrane has always resented her existence, you know, and she scarcely allowed the child to call her soul her own. I think it's that which makes her difficult at times now; and when I'm tempted to be angry with her, and deal strictly with her, I remember that."

"But other children are made to be obedient," Miss Maynard reminded her. "Where would you find parents who expect more unquestioning obedience than the Maranis? The Mensches are pretty strict, but Gisela and Maria have been taught the most unquestioning and absolute obedience. And it's the same with most of our girls — the continental ones, at any rate. I like it better than the calm disregarding of orders that one gets nowadays from children."

"So do I," returned her friend. "The trouble is that Grizel

39

was thoroughly spoilt by her grandmother for five years before her father's second marriage. Then, though our girls have been taught to obey on the word, they aren't nagged at. That's bad for anyone, and it is Mrs Cochrane's chief failing.''

"Well, what are we to do? I know that she expects to be degraded. If you think we ought to try her again, I am quite willing. Only I do hope she's learnt her lesson *this* time, and will play no more such wild pranks. I *cannot* see how any girl of eighteen can be so mad!"

Mrs Russell nodded. "I know. But it's just Grizel. I will have a talk with her, and see what she says, and, of course, we must consult Mademoiselle. Then, if you and she agree, I think we must give the child a last chance, I *don't* want to degrade her. That sort of thing sticks, and it might harm her more than it would do her good.''

The door opened at that moment, and Grizel came in. She had slipped away from the others, and had come to learn her fate. "Has Miss Maynard told you, Madame?" she faltered.

"Told me what?" asked Mrs Russell.

"About my running away to Schaffhausen? I know it was a mad thing to do, but I wanted to see the Falls of Rhine so much, and I didn't think.''

Miss Maynard got up and left the room. She felt that it would be easier for Grizel to make her confession if she were alone with the Head — for so they all thought of Mrs Russell.

"Yes, Grizel. She has told me. I am very disappointed in you.''

Grizel's lips quivered. "I'm awfully sorry, Madame. I just didn't think.''

"That is the trouble with you, Grizel," said Madge gravely as she drew the girl down on a chair beside her. "You *don't* think; and so you give everyone endless trouble. Do you think that a girl like that ought to be our head girl?"

Grizel shook her head. She couldn't speak, for she was fighting desperately for self-control.

"I want you to have another chance," said Mrs Russell quietly. "Miss Maynard and I are going to talk it over with Mademoiselle. If she agrees, we will try you for this term. But remember, Grizel, if we do, it will really be your last chance this time. I dare not hurt the school for the sake of one girl."

She dismissed the girl after that, but Grizel went away happier than she had come. She knew that kind-hearted Mademoiselle Lapâttre would agree to giving her this chance.

CHAPTER 5

The Prefects' Meeting

In the prefects' room, Grizel sat alone. It was the first Saturday of term, and she was to hold her first prefects' meeting. She had been looking forward to it, but now that it was here she felt sudden doubts as to whether she would be able to manage as well as her predecessors had done. Sitting there by herself, she went over them in her own mind. Tall, graceful Gisela, with her wide commonsense and her quiet tact, which had helped to bring her through that first test year; big, steady Juliet, who had been the Head's right hand, and the beloved of all the Juniors; pretty Bette, who had had only one term of office, but had proved in that term that she, too, possessed the something which goes to make leaders. Yes; they were a fine trio to follow, and she must work hard if she meant to rise to their level.

For once in her life Grizel saw herself with open eyes; saw how her actions really looked. She did not like it. Something foreign to it came into her face as she sat there, looking unseeingly out of the window that gave on to the long narrow valley which runs into the mountains from the shores of the Tiern See. She vowed to herself that she would make good in this term of trial. She would *not* let Mrs Russell, Miss Maynard, or Mademoiselle down, come what might. In her grim determination she clenched her hands and squared her jaw, robbing her face of half its beauty, but giving it an added character.

Well might Rosalie Dene, the second prefect, who entered the room just then, exclaim, "Grizel! What in the world has happened?"

Grizel's face resumed its normal appearance as she said hastily, "Nothing! What should have happened?"

"I don't know, I'm sure," said Rosalie, pulling up a chair to the table and sitting down. "You looked as if — as if —

oh, I don't know! As if you were declaring war on someone."

"What nonsense!" Grizel laughed.

Rosalie shot a quick glance at her, then she decided to change the subject. "Where do you think the others are? They're late!"

"Here they are," said Grizel, whose quick ear had heard the sound of light footsteps. "Come along, you people! I was beginning to think you'd forgotten all about it!"

"I am sorry," said Gertrud Steinbrücke, "I was talking with Mademoiselle about the library, and had not noticed how late it was."

"And we were getting the Middles and Juniors started with their hobbies," added Mary Burnett, a sturdy English girl, with a pleasant face and downright manner. "Jo, Paula, and Marie are looking after the little ones, and the Middles are with Eva and Dorota. Jo says, Grizel, do you want to discuss the magazine? If so she'll come. But if you don't she'll stay where she is."

Grizel thought. "No; I don't think we shall need her this afternoon," she said slowly. "We must have a meeting of the committee soon, though. Do you mind running down and telling her, Mary? Ask her to find out from the others if they can have a meeting after tea, will you?"

"Righto!" Mary went off on her errand, and the rest of the prefects and sub-prefects settled down.

They made an attractive group as they sat there. There were eight of them. Grizel was in her place at the head of the table. Next to her was Rosalie, fair, quiet, and very English-looking. On her other hand was Gertrud, who had taken her place as games captain, and below her, Luigia di Ferara, an Italian girl, who was the eldest of them all, since she would be eighteen in three weeks' time. Below these grandees sat the sub-prefects — Vanna di Ricci, another Italian girl, and a great favourite with everybody; Lisa Bernaldi, the only day-girl to be a prefect; Mary Burnett, when she should come; and Deira O'Hagan, a wild Irish girl from County Cork, whose glowing, dark prettiness told of her Spanish grandmother. Deira was something of a firebrand in the school, for she was hot-tempered, haughty, and very nearly as strong-headed as Grizel herself. The two always sparred when together. They were too much alike in character to get on well.

Mary came back presently and took her seat, and Grizel stood up to open proceedings. "This is the new term," she said slowly. "We have, unfortunately, lost Bette Rincini, who made such a splendid head girl last term, and I've got to do my best to carry on the tradition she has left. I hope you'll all help me." She paused and looked round at them all, but even Deira was smiling and nodding approval. She went on: "We had better have the report of last term now, I think, and then we can decide what we are to do this term. Rosalie, will you please read it."

She sat down, and Rosalie stood up and read out the following report. " 'Last term was a good term. The snow did not come till halfway through November, so we were able to have hockey and netball nearly the whole of the term. Inter-form matches were played, and the Sixth Form came first, with the Fourth second, the Fifth third in hockey. In netball, the Lower Fourth were first, the Second second, and the Third third. During October, a party of English school-girls were staying at the Stephanie, and they made up a team and challenged us. The game was won by the Chalet School by three goals to one.' — That was in hockey," she added, turning to the others for a minute. "They also challenged us at netball, and won by seventeen goals to twelve. 'In the Hobbies Club good work was done in handicrafts, and an exhibition was held on the last Saturday of term. The cup offered by the staff to the form that did the best and most original work went to the Fifth Form, who gained it through Frieda Mensch's dolls of all nations, and Josephine Bettany's marionette theatre which she had made herself. In the Guides, two girls, Grizel Cochrane and Mary Burnett, won the all-round cord, and Gertrud Steinbrücke, Deira O'Hagan, Josephine Bettany, Paula von Rothenfels, and Marie von

Eschenau passed the First Class test. Other Guides did well in the tests exams held at the end of term, ninety-two per cent passing in those for which they had entered. In folk dancing we all worked hard, and we learned several new dances, and also began sword dancing. We did Flamborough, and hope to do Kirkby this term. The eighth number of our magazine, the *Chaletian*, appeared and was better than ever. It has been decided to have a copy of each number bound and placed in the school library so that girls may always see how we have progressed since we began it. It was also decided to hold an Old Girls' Day once a year, and this was fixed to come in the summer term, and, if possible, on Madame's birthday, the fourth of July. Our annual Nativity play was given in the new hall, which Herr Braun had built for us during the last summer holidays, and was a great success.' That's all,'' went on Rosalie, closing the exercise book. "It was a fairly full term, though nothing like *some* we've had!''

"No floods," added Grizel; "nor any fires or raging thunderstorms. It was a dull term on the whole, wasn't it? I can't think of a single thing you've left out, Rosalie. Shall we sign it, you people?''

They all agreed, so the book was passed round, and the eight people signed the report.

The next thing was to decide what they were going to do about games for that term. Easter was always rather a difficulty for them. The first few weeks gave them ice sport, but March generally brought the spring thaw with it, and everything was muddy, and skating, skiing, and snowball fights had to be taken off the programme. On the other hand, neither netball nor hockey was possible, as the field was more or less a swamp. This meant that something else had to be provided, and it was the prefects' duty to make suggestions.

"What about tracking games?" suggested Gertrud.

"All right if the thaw is quick. If it isn't, well, it's all wrong," replied Grizel. "You know what it's like then — knee-deep in mud! Matey would have a fit if we brought the youngsters into anything of the kind. As far as that goes, she'd have a fit over any of us. The cleanest person can't help looking like a tramp after tracking through mud and puddles."

"What about rounders?" suggested Mary.

"Where's the use? If we could have rounders, we could have hockey and netball — netball, anyhow."

"I suppose it'll resolve itself into our usual walks," said Rosalie. "The Middles hate them, but it can't be helped, I suppose. That's the only drawback to living here."

"Well, it's a jolly small drawback!" declared Deira. "I'd a million times rather be at school here and put up with the thaw than be in a town — even Innsbruck!"

"All the same, I think we ought to try to think of *something* fresh," insisted Grizel. "As Rosalie says, the Middles hate walks, even when they can break rank and wander. Can't anyone think of something?"

"I have thought of something," said Lisa shyly, "but I do not know if we may do it."

"Well, let's have it, anyway," said Grizel.

"It is that perhaps we might make expeditions for geography and history at the weekend. Do you think it would be possible? We could not go every weekend, of course, but if the Middles knew that they would have a trip to Hall one Saturday to see it, and to learn all they could from it of history, do you not think they would make few objections to a walk the other Saturdays?"

"It's an idea," said Grizel slowly. "There's a good deal we could see. We ought to do Innsbruck thoroughly, you know. And then there's Salzburg. And the Stubai glacier. The only thing is, it would cost rather a lot, wouldn't it?"

"Not if we made a large party," said Vanna, joining in for the first time. "Surely we could manage it then. The big difficulty to me is how we should get to Spärtz. The railway does not open till May. We should have to walk down the mountainside, and in thaw time that would not be pleasant. Also, we could not take the Juniors."

"No, there's that to think of too. If expeditions can be arranged for the rest of the school, we must manage something for the babes," said Grizel slowly. "They could manage Innsbruck, perhaps — even Hall, they might do. But Salzburg is a longish train journey, and would tire them; and the Stubai is out of the question, of course. But it *is* an idea, and a jolly fine one. We'll see what the staff say, anyway."

"Then what can we arrange for the little ones?" asked Rosalie. "We must have something ready for them, you know, or the other idea will be squashed at once."

There was truth in what she said, and the eight girlish faces wore heavy frowns in their endeavours to settle this difficulty. One or two suggestions were made, but all had to be rejected. Some of the little ones were very little — no older than the Robin. One or two were delicate; and there was always Matron, who was a good sort but waged war on mud and dirt of all kinds. It was Mary who made the best suggestion.

"Couldn't they have little expeditions of their own? They love Spärtz. If we could get them down there they could have a good time in the gardens, and there is a good *conditorei* where they could have cakes and coffee. Then they couldn't do as much as we could in one day, so they might take two or even three over Innsbruck."

"It isn't so much the getting them there as getting them back," said Grizel thoughtfully. "It's a long pull up the mountain, and they would be tired to begin with. Even if two of the staff and a pre and a sub-pre were with them it would be a business getting them home again. People like the Robin and Paula's little sister would be done, and the staff won't agree to anything that's going to keep them in bed all next day."

Things were at an impasse, so they decided to leave the question alone and get on to the next business, which was settling duties for the term. Here the first dispute arose. Grizel as head girl had so much on her hands that she could take on nothing beyond her turn at prep and cloakroom duty.

47

Gertrud was Captain of the Games, and that would keep her occupied. Rosalie Dene agreed to undertake stationery, a task which just suited her, for she was orderly and methodical — two very necessary qualities for the work.

"Then, if I may, I will see to break, Grizel," said Lisa. "As I am here during school hours only, it will be as well for me to do that."

"It's a good deal of work," said Grizel doubtfully. "Oughtn't you to take turns with someone?"

But Lisa refused to hear of it. She had no evening duties, she said, and no morning work. She would rather do the break duties herself.

"Than Luigia, will you do library?" asked Grizel. "Joey will help you as usual, I suppose. And Vanna, you had better be music prefect again. You learn with Herr Anserl, and know just how he likes things. Plato needs looking after too," she went on, referring to their eccentric singing master. "Mary, you had better see to the form rooms, and also the staff room, if you don't mind. That leaves hobbies for you, Deira."

Mary and Vanna had agreed with nods to the duties she assigned to them, but Deira was not pleased, and took pains to let them all know at once.

"I don't want to be hobbies prefect," she said. "It's the most tiresome job of the lot, and you never get a chance to get on with your own work. I don't like it at all!" The others stared at her in undisguised amazement. So far, no one had ever objected to any duty given her by the head girl. You simply accepted what was given you, and did your best with it. When Grizel had recovered her breath she said so.

"I don't care what you've always done," said Deira calmly. "A change is a good thing sometimes, and I'm not liking the work. Why shouldn't I be music prefect?"

"'Cos Vanna is," Grizel told her. "She knows Herr Anserl, and you don't even have lessons with him. If you did you'd not be talking rubbish about wanting to have more to do with him than you could help!"

"Deira can have form rooms if she likes, and I'll do hobbies," said Mary, who was by way of being a peace-maker, and who saw that both Deira and Grizel were likely to have a quarrel if left long to themselves. "I don't mind. I'm not doing anything special this term — only going on with my stamps. You know the babes take a lot of time sometimes, and if Deira has anything extra she wants to do it would be rather a trial."

"Have you?" asked Grizel of Deira.

"No; I haven't," said Deira sulkily.

"Then you can't change, Mary. — I'm sorry you don't like being hobbies prefect, Deira, but all the other jobs are settled. Besides, anyhow, I don't see why you want to argue about it. The rule here is that the head girl settles the work."

"'Tis a rotten rule, it is, then!" responded Deira, with spirit. "I'm not agreeing with it at all, Grizel Cochrane! Why should you choose, as if we were kids?"

"Because I happen to be head girl," Grizel told her firmly.

"Don't be silly, Deira," said Rosalie. "We've always settled things this way, and no one ever made a fuss about it before. You didn't object last term yourself."

"Ah, Bette was head girl then," said Deira.

"So you're making this fuss just because *I'm* head girl now?" said Grizel. "Well, you can go on making a fuss, but you'll be hobbies prefect till the end of term. And so I tell you!"

"And I won't do it! And so I tell *you*!" retorted Deira. "'Tis a tyrant you are, Grizel Cochrane! I'm not going to put my neck under your heel!"

"Nobody asked you! Don't be so absurd!" said Grizel crossly. "And if you won't be hobbies prefect, then you won't have any job at all."

Fire flashed in Deira's grey eyes, and her face was flushed with passion. What might have happened next there is no saying, but just then the Robin knocked at the door. "Please, it is *Kaffee,* and Miss Durrant says will you have it up here, or will you come downstairs?"

49

"We'll have it up here, Robin," said Grizel. "Will two of you go and fetch it, please? Now, Deira," she went on, turning to the girl as Mary and Vanna followed the Robin out of the room. "I'm sorry I didn't know before you disliked being hobbies prefect, but it can't be helped now. Next term, if you *still* want it, you can have a shot at music; for this term the duties are arranged, and will have to stay put. I showed the list to Mademoiselle last night when Madame was down, and they both saw it, and said it was all right. Of course, they couldn't know you would object. If they had, they might have asked me to alter it! As it is, they didn't, and it's signed. Madame won't be down for a fortnight now, so it will have to stay. *Don't* do your duty if you feel all that bad about it. I dare say we can manage. But it'll be rotten of you if you don't!"

Deira turned white, and her eyes gleamed black with rage. She knew that the head girl had the whip hand. Mrs Russell was no longer working Head of the school, but she still took part in it; all lists were signed by her, and all big arrangements had to be discussed with her. Mademoiselle Lapâttre had insisted on that before she had agreed to become the nominal Head. If Madame, as they still loved to call her, were not coming from the Sonnalpe for a fortnight, then the lists must remain as she had passed them. All the same, Deira was very angry. She had protested, not so much because she disliked the work, as because she objected to Grizel's rather dictatorial manner. Her protest had not worked, but she loved Grizel none the better for that.

"If I must, I must," she choked out at length. "All the same, Grizel Cochrane, I'll be even with you yet!"

"Rats!" said Grizel briefly, and began to discuss other duties with them as if nothing had happened.

Mary and Vanna brought in *Kaffee und Kuchen,* their afternoon meal, and they were all too busy settling days and work to notice how silently the Irish girl sat through their discussion. She drank her coffee and ate the cakes they passed her without realizing what she was eating or drinking. Her temper was aroused, and she was resolved to make Grizel Cochrane smart for what she had said.

When the meeting had ended, and Lisa had gone home with her father, most of the prefects went off to their dormitories to change into light frocks, as they were going to dance that evening. Grizel was left behind, and Gertrud stayed with her.

"I wish you had not spoken to Deira quite as you did, Grizel," said the Austrian girl rather nervously, for she did *not* like speaking about it at all to Grizel, who was quite likely to turn on her.

Grizel looked at her frowningly. "I rather wish I hadn't myself," she owned; "but she does rile me so! After all, Gertrud, I couldn't have given in. It isn't the way we do things."

"No; but you were very sarcastic," said Gertrud bravely. "She is angry, Grizel."

"Well, let's hope she gets over it quickly," said Grizel. "Oh, Gertrud, I wish Bette had stayed on! I didn't want to be head girl one bit! But if I'm it, I'll *be* it!"

Gertrud said nothing. There seemed to be nothing to say.

Grizel slipped an arm through hers. "Gertrud, I couldn't alter things like that! You *do* agree with me there, don't you?"

"Oh, yes; I agree with that," said Gertrud readily. "But Grizel, Deira is very angry, and she does bad things when she is angry. She is sorry after, I know; but it never stops her from doing them the next time she is — how do you call it? — upset."

Grizel stood still, a funny look on her face. This description might have fitted her. "Well," she said finally. "I will try to keep out of her way and not make things worse."

She wished she had kept her temper, and *not* been sarcastic about those lists.

CHAPTER 6

Deira Gets Her Own Back

"Has anyone seen my manuscript book?" asked Grizel Cochrane abruptly, coming into the big form room on Sunday afternoon.

The Middles, who were all there, stared.

"Your manuscript book, Grizel? No, I haven't," said Margia Stevens at length. "When did you have it last?"

"It was in my music locker on Friday," replied Grizel. "I put it away just before afternoon school, and I slipped a letter from home into it. Now I can't find it, and I want it — at least I want that letter."

"Did you have a letter? Lucky you!" said Margia.

"It was an old one," said Grizel briefly. "Haven't any of you seen the wretched thing?"

They all assured her that they did not, so she went off to hunt through all the lockers in case she had slipped her book into the wrong one. Mademoiselle came along and stopped in astonishment at the sight. "Grizel!" she cried in her own language, "what are you doing here?"

"I am looking for my manuscript book, Mademoiselle," explained Grizel, lifting a flushed face.

"But this is Sunday! You cannot do harmony on Sunday!" protested Mademoiselle.

"Oh, it wasn't for that I wanted it," said Grizel, rising from her knees to stand before the nominal Head of the school. "I left a letter in it, and I want the letter. I thought I had put the book into my locker, but it isn't there, so I was looking to see if I had made a mistake and put it into someone else's, as I was in rather a hurry."

"Yes, *ma petite*; in that case you may look for the book," said Mademoiselle, passing on and leaving Grizel to go on with her hunt — a fruitless hunt, as it proved to be.

Wherever that book was, it wasn't in the music lockers.

Finally Grizel gave it up and went to turn out her desk though she was certain she had not carried her harmony into form with her.

Gertrud came in as she was busy, and opened her eyes widely.

"It's my wretched manuscript book," explained Grizel once more as she ran through a pile of exercise books. "I simply can't find the thing! It seems to have vanished off the face of the earth!"

"But harmony!" protested Gertrud.

The rule about work on Sunday was strictly kept at the Chalet School. No lessons at all might be done then. In the mornings the girls went to the little Roman Catholic chapel if there was a service — all of them that were Catholics, that is. The rest had a service of their own in one of the form rooms. In the afternoon they were free to amuse themselves with books, puzzles, or painting. The little ones had to lie down for an hour. After *Kaffee und Kuchen*, Mademoiselle took the Catholics, and Miss Maynard had the English Church girls for an hour, and they had quiet talks together. After that they were free once more till bedtime. Margia Stevens in her first term at the school had told her mother that they had "such gentle Sundays". The girls were never likely to forget their Sundays at the Chalet School. Hence Gertrud's surprise at Grizel's statement.

The head girl knew what was passing in her mind. "Oh, it isn't harmony; only I left a letter of Grannie's — the last she ever wrote me — in it, and I want that letter."

Gertrud's pretty face softened. Everyone knew that Grizel had loved her grandmother, who had died two years previously, and who had adored and petted her. She kept that particular letter because in it was a good deal of gentle, loving advice which she very seldom followed, it is true, but which she liked nevertheless.

"Perhaps the book has been taken to our room," suggested Gertrud practically, that being the only sort of sympathy Grizel would permit. "Shall I go and see?"

53

"It's awfully good of you, but I think I'll go myself. Come, though, if you like."

Gertrud slipped an arm through her friend's, and they went upstairs together. In the prefects' room they found Vanna, who was writing letters, and Deira, who was reading. The Irish girl scowled as the two came in, and turned her back on them. Vanna, deep in her home letter, took no notice of them as they hunted through the cupboard and then went through the long, low bookshelves that ran along the wall at one side.

"It isn't here," said Gertrud at length, when the most consistent search had proved that, wherever the missing book was, it wasn't in the room.

"Where on earth can it be?" said Grizel, a puzzled frown on her face. "I'm *sure* I put it into my locker, because I remember I had finished all my harmony for Herr Anserl, and I put it there to be ready for Monday. If I bring it up here, I nearly always forget to take it to my lesson, and nothing makes him madder than to wait while I go and fetch it. I *know* I put it there with my music; and now it's gone!"

"Perhaps it has fallen out and been put into lost property," suggested Gertrud.

"It might. I'll go and see. Who has the key? Whose week is it?"

"Deira's," said Gertrud, after a glance at the neatly written list on the notice board.

Grizel turned to Deira. "Deira, may I have the key to lost property?" she said.

"It's hanging up beside the board there," mumbled Deira, not looking up from her book.

Grizel, thinking that Deira was still angry over yesterday, took no notice of her manner, but got the key and went off. Gertrud did, however, and remained where she was, looking at the Irish girl with a frown. Grizel came back in five minutes' time, empty-handed, and hung up the key on its nail. "No; it wasn't there," she said. "I can't imagine where it can have got to."

"What are you looking for?" asked Vanna, who had been roused out of her letter by this time, and was taking an interest in the proceedings.

"My harmony book. You haven't seen it, by any chance?"

"No; not since you had it on Friday," said Vanna. "But harmony, Grizel?"

"It's the book I want. There's an old letter in it — that's all."

At this Deira started and went white.

Gertrud noticed it. "Deira, have you seen Grizel's book?" she asked.

Deira faced her and remained silent. She hardly dared tell the truth, and she could not lie over the matter.

Grizel's attention was now attracted. "Deira! Do you know where it is?" she asked sharply.

"Not now," said Deira, almost inaudibly.

"Not now? What on earth d'you mean?" demanded Grizel impatiently.

Her impatience had one good effect. It made Deira speak up. "I meant what I said. I haven't the least idea where it is at the moment. On the ash-heap, I should think."

"The ash-heap? What on earth are you talking about?" Grizel had gone paler, and her eyes were beginning to look steely.

"Well, isn't that where the ashes are thrown?" Deira spoke defiantly but inwardly she was feeling anything but defiant.

"Ashes? D'you mean you've *burnt* it?" Grizel was white now, and her lips were set in a thin straight line. Deira felt frightened; however, she wasn't going to let Grizel Cochrane know it, so she shrugged her shoulders.

"If you know, why ask?"

"You've *burnt* it?" repeated Grizel, as if she could scarcely believe her ears.

"Yes, I've burnt it! I vowed I'd make you pay for your sarcasm yesterday, and I have! It's fine and early you'll have to be getting up tomorrow, if you want to get that harmony done again before your lesson!"

"Deira! But how *could* you?" cried Gertrud. "It was a wicked thing to do! And you have burnt Grizel's letter too! Her letter that she cherished!"

"Oh, dry up!" said Grizel impatiently. "What does it matter about the letter now it's gone? As for the book, Deira O'Hagan, what right had you to burn school property to satisfy your silly temper? Of all childish things to do, I must say that strikes me as *the* most childish I've ever heard of! The Robin wouldn't do a mad thing like that! Oh, I shan't tell!" with unutterable scorn in her voice. "You needn't be afraid of *that*—!"

"I'm not afraid!" retorted Deira. "If it comes to that, I'll tell myself!"

"Yes; I can see you!" Grizel was realizing her loss, and her hot temper boiled up. "Dash off to Mademoiselle's room now, and tell her that you lost your temper, and did a thoroughly childish, spiteful thing like that just to work it off! I can see you!"

"I will! Do you suppose I care for you, Grizel Cochrane?" raged Deira.

"Girls! What does this mean?" Miss Maynard had come into the room after vainly rapping for admittance, since everyone was too much interested in what was going on to heed anything else.

At the mistress's words Gertrud looked distressed, and Vanna frightened. Grizel uttered a scornful laugh and turned away. Deira, stung to utter fury by that laugh, sprang forward. "I have been telling Grizel Cochrane what I think of her, Miss Maynard," she exploded, becoming more and more Irish as she went on. "'Tis not meself would be afraid of her, for all the haughty airs of her. And, since actions spake louder than words, I been telling her 'tis I have burnt her harmony book!"

"You've — *what*! exclaimed Miss Maynard, startled out of her usual self-possession.

"I've burnt her harmony book," repeated Deira, still too angry to care what happened.

56

"*Deira*! Are you mad?"

Deira treated this as if it had never been uttered and swept on, "'Tis not meself'll be submitting to the tyranny of her, be she fifty times head girl here. She may be English — the curse of Cromwell on thim all!" (this last with a sudden hazy remembrance of her old nurse) — "but I'm Irish, and there's niver a one of us fears the tyrant—"

But by this time Miss Maynard had recovered herself, and she interrupted what promised to be a long harangue on the wrongs of Ireland. "Deira, leave the room at once — at once! Go to your dormitory, and don't leave it till I give you permission."

Deira glared at her, but Miss Maynard was to be obeyed, and the look the excited girl received from the mistress helped to cool her down considerably. She turned and went without another word. Miss Maynard waited till she had gone, and then attended to Grizel. "Grizel, will you kindly explain to me the meaning of this *disgraceful* scene? What has happened between you and Deira?"

Grizel shook her head. Tell tales she would not; also, she was too angry to speak.

Seeing how matters stood, Miss Maynard turned to Gertrud. "Gertrud, you seem to have kept your head. Will you please tell me what this is all about?"

"Grizel and Deira had quarrelled," said Gertrud, after a moment's pause. "Deira has burnt Grizel's harmony."

"Is it really true? She really has done such a childish thing?"

"Yes." Poor Gertrud felt miserable over the whole thing.

Miss Maynard stood in silence for a moment. "Why has she done this, Grizel?"

"Deira didn't like all the arrangements yesterday," mumbled Grizel at last, when she had kept the mistress waiting as long as she dared. "I made her angry, and this is to pay me out, I suppose."

"How did you make her angry?"

"I — said things."

Miss Maynard forbore to question further. She sent Grizel off downstairs to the others, and managed to get a more detailed account from Vanna and Gertrud. She got more than she had bargained for; for Vanna, thoroughly frightened, told about the precious letter that must have gone, too, and this helped to explain Grizel's attitude. When the young mistress had finally got everything there was to get she went off to Mademoiselle to report to her.

"And now, what are we to do?" she asked when she had finished.

Poor Mademoiselle put her hand to her head. "I cannot think. I only wish our dear Marguérite had never left us and got married. How to deal with this extraordinary happening I do not know. Deira must be punished, of course, but I fear that will do little good. It will not make her really repentant for what she had done, nor will it return the letter. As for what Herr Anserl will say when he hears about the harmony, I shudder to think!"

"He'll roar, I suppose," agreed Miss Maynard. "He always is noisy over things like that. But Grizel certainly can't get all that work done over again in time."

"Doubtless, my dear Mollie," replied Mademoiselle dryly; "but that will not help us in dealing with the matter. Here comes Marie with the coffee. We had better try to forget it for the time being, and take our rest while we can. As for Deira, she had better stay by herself. Will you go and ask Matron to put her in the sick room for the rest of today. She will be better left alone, I think, till she has had time to realize what she has done."

CHAPTER 7

A Deadlock

"Here's Madame at last!" The cry came from Grizel, who had been anxiously watching the mountain path along which their ex-headmistress must come to reach the school. Things were uncomfortable, and had been since that memorable Sunday. Deira had been allowed to join the rest of the school the next day, but she kept by herself, speaking to no one.

"What to do, I know not," said Mademoiselle, speaking to a conclave of Miss Maynard, Miss Durrant, who was the junior mistress, and Miss Wilson, who taught general subjects.

"We had better send for Madame, I think," said Miss Wilson thoughtfully.

Miss Maynard shook her head. "I don't think we ought to bother her, if we can help it. The Sonnalpe is a good way away for a tramp in this weather" — it was snowing heavily, and threatening to become a blizzard before long — "the paths won't be safe. Also, I do think we ought to settle our own difficulties."

Luckily for them all, Mrs Russell sent a message to say that she was coming down to see Joey, so the matter had been shelved for the time being. Deira found herself left severely alone by the others, and Grizel, anxious to do her best to prove to "Madame" that she had been justified in her forgiveness by being an excellent head girl, had worried from morning till night about the trouble in the school.

She had done what she could to set matters right. She spoke to the Irish girl as nicely as if she had done nothing — which further enraged Deira, who was under the impression that Grizel's attitude meant that she didn't care — and fulfilled all her duties as carefully as she could. Joey even accused her of becoming old-maidish.

When at length the day Mrs Russell had fixed for her

coming arrived, Grizel spent all her spare time at the window, watching. Joey and the Robin joined her halfway through break, and the three of them were in the prefects' room, staring up the valley, when the head girl's joyful exclamation told them that their expected visitor was coming. Joey promptly made for the door, closely followed by the Robin. Grizel waited by herself. Slowly, very slowly, she was beginning to see things from other people's point of view, and she knew that the three would prefer to have their first meeting in privacy.

As it happened, they were all doomed to disappointment, for the bell rang just then, and all three had to go to classes. The Robin heaved a sigh, and trotted off to her own quarters at Le Petit Chalet, the Junior house. Joey turned aside from the passage, and went to her form room, where she proceeded to display the most remarkable ignorance of the doings of Louis the Ninth and his Crusaders; and Grizel went down to the Sixth, and tried to forget her troubles in German literature and *Wilhelm Meister*.

Meantime the person so eagerly looked for went quietly up the snowy path to the house, where she was welcomed by Mademoiselle, who drew her into the little room still known as "Madame's study", and rang the bell for Luise, the maid, to bring *Kaffee und Brödchen*.

"Oh, but it's good to be back, Elise!" sighed Mrs Russell, leaning back in her chair and looking round the familiar room with tender eyes. "I am as happy as can be at the Sonnalpe, but I do miss my girls at times."

"But you are happy, *ma Mie*?" queried Mademoiselle. "You would not be without *Monsieur le Docteur*?"

Madge shook her head. "Oh, no! But the Chalet School is part of me still. You don't know how much I sometimes wish I could be in both places at once! If only Jem could have built his sanatorium down here it would have been ideal. But the Sonnalpe is better for his work, and — and I wouldn't really change, even to be Madge Bettany of the Chalet School again."

Luise entered at this moment with the little meal, and the two joined in it and more school gossip till the bell rang for the end of morning school. Then Mademoiselle rose, "You will excuse that I run away, *ma petite*. There are one or two little things to which I must attend before *Mittagessen*. I will send Jo to you."

She went off, and three minutes later Joey appeared and hugged her sister tempestuously. "Madge! It's just like old times seeing you here! It was rotten of the bell to ring just when we saw you coming! How long are you going to stay?"

"Three days," replied her sister. "Jem has had to go off to Vienna again, so I said I'd rather come here till he comes back. Now, tell me your news."

"Except for this idiotic fuss with Deira and Grizel, I don't think there *is* any," replied Jo, rumpling up her hair with her hand.

"Fuss with Deira and Grizel? *What* fuss?" asked her sister sharply.

"Oh, it isn't Grizel's fault," declared Joey. "She's been jolly decent about it all. Only Deira went mad and burned her harmony, and her grannie's last letter with it!"

"*What*? Sit down, and tell me what it all means!" commanded Madge.

"I can't tell you much more. Deira had a row of sorts with Grizel — don't know what about, though. You know what Deira is. She lost her temper, and tried to pay Grizel out by burning her things. *I* think it was an utterly mad thing to do and she doesn't seem to care, either! Grizel has been jolly nice about it, and I know she was upset about the letter. No one can do anything with Deira, and she mopes about all day by herself. None of us want to talk to her, though we're polite, of course. Deira won't say she's sorry, and it's been jolly unpleasant!"

Madge Russell turned matters over in her own mind. She felt glad, on the whole, that she had decided against accompanying her husband to Vienna. During the three days she would be at the school surely she could clear up this trouble. Not unnaturally, she felt inclined to blame Grizel herself in the first instance. It seemed almost certain that she had brought this trouble on herself.

Joey, watching her sister's face, guessed what was passing through her mind, and tried to put matters as straight as she could. "Madge, I don't think this is Grizel's fault. In fact, the other prefects practically say it isn't, though they won't tell *us* what's happened. Grizel has been awfully upset about it all, and she's done her best to straighten it up — honour bright, she has. Only, Deira doesn't seem to want it straightened."

Madge frowned. "Sure of this, Joey?"

"Positive certain," declared Joey. "Do believe that it isn't her fault, Madge."

"Do you think I'm condemning her unheard?" asked her sister dryly. "You've never called me unfair before, Joey."

Joey crimsoned. "No; but I think — things — make you feel that — that — that—"

"That — what?" demanded Mrs Russell, as the orator came to a distressed halt.

"Well, that it is more likely to be her fault than Deira's."

Madge Russell looked at her sister again. Then she nodded. "You're right, Joey — and it *is* unfair!"

"I didn't say so!"

"Not exactly. But you *meant* it, didn't you?"

Jo fidgetted. Then she looked up. "Yes, I think I did. I can't bear you to be wrong in anything!"

"I'm often wrong, Joey-baba," sighed her sister, an arm round the slender shoulders. "I certainly was there! Listen! Here comes the Robin!"

Joey wriggled away, and stood up as the Robin came racing into the room and flung herself on "Tante Marguérite" with cries of joy. "Tante Guito! How lovely to have you again! School isn't so nice without you!"

Mrs Russell kissed the rosy face upturned to hers, and ruffled the short curls as she said, "You have me in the holidays, *Bübchen*."

"That's not the same," said the Robin sagely. "We want you all the time — Joey an' me!"

"And I want you! Are you being a very good girl, sweetheart?"

"I was second — but *second* in my form last week," said the Robin impressively. "And I have no order marks all this term!"

"Papa will be pleased to hear that. He sent his love to you, my pet, and when Uncle Jem comes home again he will come down for a weekend at the Post, and you and Joey are to stay with him."

The Robin squeezed her hands together in her joy. "But that will be *jolly*!" she said emphatically.

"Wonderful!" Jo added her comment. "Will it be next weekend, Madge?"

"Yes, I think so. And I am here for three days this time, Robin; and I am going to ask Mademoiselle if I may take my classes again. She tells me that Miss Annersley has a bad cold, so we will send her to the sick room, and give her a rest while I am here."

The Robin hugged her again as the only possible means of expressing her joy, and the bell rang for *Mittagessen* just when everyone was nicely tousled, for Joey had joined in the hug. They made a frantic rush for the Splasheries on that, and the two children had to run, while Mrs Russell followed more soberly to the staff room, where she was greeted with acclamations as the staff filed out to go to the *Speisesaal*.

"You will take your own seat, Madame?" said Mademoiselle, who was already in her old place, leaving the head of the staff table to the younger woman. Mrs Russell nodded, and went there. Then she said grace, and they all sat down.

It was like old times to sit there, looking down the room at the long tables with the fresh faces turning to her; and yet there were differences. Gisela, Bernhilda, Juliet, Wanda, and Bette were no longer there. Grizel Cochrane sat in the head girl's seat, dispensing the soup to the little ones, and Joey was no longer a child. Others had grown up, too, and there were new faces among the little ones. Particularly, Mrs Russell noticed Grizel and Deira. The former looked grave and preoccupied, and the latter was plainly miserable. She merely played with her food, and made no attempt to join in the merry chattering in which even Frölich Armundsen, a new little Norwegian, was managing to take part, though it was French day, and till she came to the school she had never heard a word of French.

Mademoiselle's eyes followed Madge's, and she looked very serious, though she said nothing. When the meal was over, however, she caught Deira outside, and brought her back to insist on her eating some of the soup which Luise had kept warm. "You must eat, Deira," she said firmly. "You will make yourself ill if you do not, and that I cannot permit."

Deira took it then, but with a very ill-used air. She escaped as soon as she could, and went off to her own quarters, feeling that the whole world was against her.

Madge Russell had gone up to the prefects' room, meanwhile, and was having a chat with her girls, who rejoiced loudly when she told them that she was going to teach during her visit.

"Oh, Madame! But that will be so nice!" cried Luigia. "It will be as it was before."

"I am so glad," said Rosalie. "We do miss you, Madame."

"What books shall we need?" asked Mary Burnett. "It's literature for us first lesson this afternoon?"

A shout of laughter rose at this; even Grizel joining in.

"But how like Mary!" chuckled Gertrud. "You are in haste to begin, my dear."

"Well, it's better not to waste any time," said Mary in her matter-of-fact way.

"Shall it be Shakespeare?" asked Vanna. "It is so long since we had a Shakespeare lesson with you, Madame."

"Yes, if you like," said Madge. "What are you doing this term?"

"*The Tempest,*" said Rosalie. "We're just finishing the first act."

"Very well, then. Bring your *Tempests.*"

Grizel produced hers from the shelf, and the others made haste to find theirs. While they were busy, the head girl turned to the ex-Head of the school. "Madame, may I speak to you after school? I do want a talk."

Mrs Russell looked at her thoughtfully. "Yes, Grizel. Come to my study and have *Kaffee* with me, will you? I shall be alone."

"Thank you," murmured Grizel. "It is good of you. I do want a talk with you."

Madge looked at her anxiously. The girl was paler than usual, and there were shadows under her eyes. She had been taking this thing badly.

"I am sure you are working well in all ways this term, Grizel," said Mrs Russell gently. "I can see that for myself."

The colour touched Grizel's face, but she said nothing more, and the return of the others waving their books put an end to the conversation.

From the Sixth, which numbered six girls only, Mrs Russell went on to the Fourth, which was the largest form in the school, and there she received a rapturous welcome. The afternoon finished up in the First, where the babies, as the older girls called them, were having "At the Back of the North Wind" read to them, with explanations where they were needed.

When the last school bell rang the few day-girls went off to get ready for their walk to the various chalets round the lake where they lived; and Mrs Russell retired to her old bedroom, changed her frock and brushed out her pretty curly hair. Then she went down to the study, where she was waylaid by Jo, who wanted to know if she and the Robin might come to *Kaffee.*

Madge shook her head. "I'm sorry, Joey, but Grizel is coming, and I want to see her alone."

Joey's face fell grievously. "Oh, Madge! We do so want to be with you!"

"I shall go over to put the Robin to bed," said her sister quietly. "You may come to my room early tomorrow morning."

"Righto, then," said Jo reluctantly. "But it's rotten luck all the same!"

"Can't help that," said Madge austerely. "Grizel needs me more than you do just now. Run along! You shall have your innings tomorrow morning."

Joey went off, fairly contented with this promise, and her sister went into the study. Grizel put in an appearance three minutes later, and then Luise arrived with *Kaffee und Kuchen*, and they were left alone.

Grizel started the ball. She took her coffee from the Head, accepted a cake, and then said nervously. "Have you heard of what has happened, Madame?"

"Do you mean between you and Deira? Yes; Jo told me."

A silence followed. Then the girl set down her coffee and turned to the Head. "Madame, on my honour as a Guide, I *have* tried!"

Madge looked her full in the face, but the grey eyes never dropped beneath hers, so she said. "Give me your version of the story, Grizel. I want to know everyone's side before I say anything."

Grizel told her story, and told it very fairly. She admitted that Deira had "made her wild", and she had been sarcastic about it. "But I never meant to make her as mad as this," she concluded. "I'm sorry, Madame."

Madge looked at her thoughtfully. "You don't realize what a bitter tongue you have when you are roused, Grizel," she said. "I am not excusing Deira's action. It was a piece of most unpleasant revenge, and thoroughly childish into the bargain. But what I want you to realize is that you are by no means blameless. I shall not say any more. I think you have suffered over this, and there is no need for anything else. I want to tell you now that if you only go on as you have been doing lately, I shall be quite satisfied to have you as head girl. As for Deira, I will see her presently, and try

66

to put this right. Now, tell me what you have been doing in games so far.''

After that she kept the talk to the games till it was time for Grizel to take prep. She sent the girl off, a different being from the one who had come in at half-past four, and asked her to tell one of the Middles to send Deira to her.

Grizel went, happier than she had been since the beginning of term, and for a few minutes Mrs Russell was alone. She got up and wandered round the room, examining her old treasures, till a tap sounded at the door. In answer to her call it opened, and Deira came in.

It was easy to see that the girl was in a bad mood. She dropped her regulation curtsey, and then stood with a defiant air.

''Come and sit down, Deira,'' said Mrs Russell cheerily, though she was far from feeling it.

Deira sat down on the edge of a chair, and waited for what was to come.

Madge Russell promptly tackled her with, ''Well, are you happy this term?''

''I'm all right,'' said Deira sulkily.

''Are you *really* happy, Deira?'' repeated the low, musical voice.

Deira sat struggling hard for self-control. She won it, and as her eyes hardened, Madge realized that it was going to be no easy matter to put things right.

''I'm as happy as I want to be,'' she said.

''You are easily satisfied,'' said the Head. Then leaning forward, ''Deira, you are *not* happy. No girl could be after doing what you have done. Why did you do it, child? What has Grizel done to you to make you feel like this towards her?''

Deira shut her lips firmly, and sat in stolid silence. Mrs Russell tried every means in her power to get her to talk, but she obstinately refused to say a word. Finally, the Head had to give it up. But she had learnt enough to know that in this instance Grizel was comparatively blameless, and she wondered that the English girl had managed to show such patience and forbearance.

"You may go, Deira," she said at length. "I am disappointed in you."

Deira went — and stood not upon the order of her going. She just managed to get up to her cubicle before her self-control vanished, and, lying on her bed, she cried heartbrokenly. That last sentence of the Head's had cut home. She would have given anything to have been able to go back to the study and say she was sorry for it all. But she felt she could not do that — yet.

The devil of pride was having it all his own way with poor Deira.

CHAPTER 8

The Snow Fight

The wind, which had been heavy, died down during the night, and frost set in. Joey Bettany, waking at the unearthly hour of five, tumbled out of bed to look out at the starry sky, and saw the white and silver tracery on the windows, which told that the earth was in an iron grip which was likely to continue for the next few weeks. By dint of breathing hard on the panes and rubbing the place with the corner of her dressing-gown, she managed to make a peep-hole for herself, and to view the landscape. The snow lay white and sparkling under the light of the dying moon, and the brilliance of the stars was a good omen. "Thanks be!" she breathed, as she got back into bed after a look at her watch to reassure herself that it was much too early to go to Madge. "Now we'll get out for a bit!"

She lay awake, for she dared not switch on the light, or she would have awakened the others. However, she had plenty to think about. She was in the middle of writing an exciting story about the Napoleonic wars, and she wanted to think out her next chapter. For the first time in her life she was finding her work difficult. The characters would not do as she wanted. They insisted on going their own sweet way, and the story was developing on quite other lines than she had intended. "I can't think what's wrong with the silly things!" she grumbled under her breath. "Why can't they do as I want? They seem to go in all directions!"

It was, had she but known it, a very promising sign. Her paper children were becoming real. It is only when a story tells itself that it is worth much.

Jo lay quite happily planning the deeds of her hero, little realizing that when it came to writing them down they would work out differently, and cause her endless trouble and annoyance. The minute she heard the clock chime six she scrambled out of bed again, and struggled into her dressing-gown. Then, with her electric torch to light the way, she tiptoed out of the room and up the stairs to the room where her sister lay, dreaming happily of her absent husband.

Madge was rudely awakened by cold feet wriggling down beside her, and she sat upright in the shock of the moment.

"All right; it's only me," said Joey in carefully guarded tones. "Lie down again, Madge. I've come for a chat."

"Did you put on your bedroom slippers?" demanded Madge, as she lay down with a caution justified by the narrowness of the bed, and put an arm round her sister.

"I did; but it's freezing like everything. Shouldn't wonder if the wolves don't come out on the plains again. They did that first winter we were here. 'Member?"

"Yes, I do! For goodness' sake keep your feet to yourself, and get them warm! They're like lumps of ice! And so are your hands!" as she encountered one of them.

"All right! I'll warm up soon. Have you got enough bed?"

"Yes; heaps! Have you? For goodness' sake, don't fall out, and waken everyone."

Jo chuckled as she snuggled closer to her sister. "They'd get a shock! Maynie's beneath. She'd think it was a young earthquake!"

Madge gurgled in company as she wriggled herself comfortable. "That's better! You're still on the bony side, Jo! I wish you'd fatten up a little!"

"Oh, I'm as fat as I want to be," returned Joey easily. "I should hate to be square — like Mary, fr'instance."

"Mary's not *fat*. She's built that way."

"Well, *I'm* not fat cos I'm built *that* way — sort of sylph-like, you know!"

Madge buried her face in the pillow to stifle her laughter. Joey was straight and thin. "Sylph-like" was the last expression one would have used to describe her. She was much too bony.

"Well, I'd rather be scraggy than tubby!" declared the insulted lady. "And *you* can't talk, anyway! There's nothing chubby about *you*, my lamb."

"Chubby? Well, I should think not!" Madge, whose round slenderness certainly gave no evidence of fat, sounded indignant.

"Keep your hair on! I said you aren't!"

"Jo, do you think we could manage a snow fight this morning?"

"Rather!" Jo was wide-awake in a minute. "What a tremendous idea! D'you really think we could?"

"Well, I don't see why not. You people have been shut up closely since term began. It will be as well to make the most of the fine weather, for one never knows how soon it may begin to snow again. I think we'll cut lessons, and stay out most of the morning. Skating will be out of the question, I'm afraid, as the ice will be too rough for it yet. A snow fight seems the best thing. You'll have to keep moving, you know."

"Righto! The others'll love it, of course!"

They discussed the idea for a short while, then Joey drifted off into other things, and they talked till the rising bell went.

At *Frühstück* it required no penetration for her to know that Joey had already passed on her idea of the snow fight to as many of her friends as possible. There was an air of excitement about the Middles, and they giggled and murmured together as much as they dared or were able. When all conversation has to be in a language foreign to some, at least, views are apt to remain rather limited in expression. Still, they made quite noise enough, and Mrs Russell rather wished that she had warned Jo to say nothing till the whole school was told. It was too late now, however, and the table was lively, to say the least of it.

None of the Seniors knew, for Jo had not mentioned it to them. They looked mildly surprised at the animation of their juniors, and Grizel began to wear a worried air. She knew that this sort of thing generally preceded a piece of outrageous naughtiness. The Head decided to keep them all in suspense no longer, so when grace had been said she checked them as they were about to leave the room, and told them what she proposed. Everyone was delighted, of course, and they raced away to make their beds, chattering gaily, while the staff congregated round the empty tables and discussed the affair a little further. It was decided that the babies were to have their own snow fight in front of Le Petit Chalet, as the older ones might be unintentionally rough. The others were to divide into two camps, one captained by Grizel, the other by Gertrud.

"Let them stay out as long as they want — or can," said Mrs Russell, with a glance at the barometer, which was very low. "We must be about to send in anyone who gets tired, of course. Some of them can't stand as much as the others. Mademoiselle and Miss Durrant will look after the Juniors, and they can all have a good time. I believe our trouble with Deira will be straightened after she has had a good two hours or so of exercise in the open air. The confinement of the last few weeks has probably helped to upset her."

"Quite likely," said Miss Maynard. "I only hope it is so. Well, shall we go and do what we have to do? The girls won't be long now."

Half an hour later the whole party was ready to go out. Everyone was well wrapped up, and everyone wore stout boots, with heavily nailed soles. They rushed out, shouting and laughing.

It was very silent outside, and a heavy grey sky showed that the snow would soon be falling again. From Le Petit Chalet there came the sound of the Juniors' voices as they tumbled about, laughing and dancing, and making snowballs. Mrs Russell left the girls, to go and see that they were all right, and Miss Maynard and Miss Wilson set to work to get the sides organized. Grizel and Gertrud had "picked up" in the house, so the two parties separated, and were each given a part of what was the flower garden in summer. They were to settle their own tactics, and the one that was driven from its own part was to be accounted the vanquished side. Several of the youngest girls were busy making snowballs, piling them up ready, while the Seniors directed their movements. Gertrud, anxious to keep the peace as far as possible, had chosen Deira for her own side, and now set her to overseeing the efforts of the Middles, while she herself posted various people at different places along her front. Then the battle began, and raged furiously. The mistresses had their work cut out to keep out of the line of fire, and yet be on the spot to see that no accidents happened.

Joey Bettany, fighting for Grizel, slipped in the snow, and went down with a wild yell, which was echoed by two of the enemy, who promptly bombarded her, so that it was some time before she was able to struggle to her feet again. Frieda Mensch, caught by Paula von Rothenfels of the other side, had her face well scrubbed in the snow before she managed to retaliate in the same way. The shouting became more and more breathless, and the laughter shriller, as the excited girls rushed and swooped, and flung handfuls of snow at each other. The dry powder could hurt no one, and the balls were not hard, so it was all very good fun. Even Deira lost her sullen air, and dashed about and shouted as hard as anyone.

Grizel, leading her side, and gradually forcing the other from its place, seemed to be everywhere at once. Now she was driving one of the enemy away; now she was rescuing one of her followers; now she was hurling snowballs as hard as she could go at her foes. One struck Deira in the face, though, as a matter of fact, it had been aimed at Gertrud. Gertrud, however, had dodged, and the snow passed by her, and caught Deira. The girl was already excited by the exercise. She scarcely knew what she was doing. To her eyes it looked as though Grizel had taken deliberate aim at her. She stooped, and grabbed at something which was lying on the ground, and had been turned up in the scrimmage. Without hesitating one second, giving herself no time to realize what it was or what she was doing, she flung it with a sure aim, and caught the other side's leader full on the temple.

Grizel flung up her hands, and gave a little cry, and went down.

At first it was looked on as a joke. It was only when Grizel lay there horribly still and silent that they realized that something had happened. The fight stopped at once. Gertrud dropped the ball she had poised to hurl at Jo, and hurried to the other girl's side. Miss Maynard raced across the garden and dropped on her knees. Grizel lay quite still, her face as white as the snow, and a thin trickle of blood showing where the missile, whatever it was, had struck her. The mistress wiped it gently away, and her lips tightened as she saw the nasty cut.

"Go and get one of your mattresses, girls," she said quietly. "Joey, go and ask Madame to come here; she is over at Le Petit Chalet. Gertrud, bring me the brandy from Matron, and ask her to get a bed ready at once. The rest of you go in, all except Mary Burnett, Rosalie Dene, Deira O'Hagan, and Eva von Heiling. Luigia, will you please take charge till someone comes?"

They did as they were told at once. Joey shot off like an arrow to fetch her sister; Gertrud went to tell Matron; and two more of the Seniors rushed up to the nearest dormitory to get a mattress. Mrs Russell had come by the time they returned with it, and was kneeling by the side of the unconscious girl. Except for the little group round Grizel, the garden was deserted now. By Grizel's side lay what had caused the accident — a sharp piece of stone, which Deira in her blind fury had flung without noticing what it was. She stood amongst the others, very white and frightened. No one, of course, had any idea that she had done it. In the heat of the battle her action had passed unnoticed. But she knew herself, and was already in an agony of remorse. They got Grizel on to the mattress, and then the girls named by Miss Maynard, helped by the staff who were there, slowly lifted it, and the girl was borne off to the sick room, where Matron, calm and capable, already had a bed opened for her, and dressing ready for the wounds. Miss Wilson went off to ring up Dr Jem to bring him posthaste, while Mrs Russell and Miss Maynard did what they could for the girl.

They had got her undressed and into bed, when she began to moan, and Madge Russell turned to her colleague. "Mollie, go and tell the girls that she is alive. I dare do nothing more till Jem comes — I don't know enough about it. It has been a near thing, though, and I'm afraid of concussion."

Miss Maynard went off to relieve the anxious girls, who were in the big classroom, talking in subdued tones. Deira was there too. She heard what the mistress said, and her white face became whiter. Miss Maynard, preoccupied and worried, never noticed her. She gave Mrs Russell's message, and left the room. Outside, in the passage, she was startled to feel a tense, nervous grip on her arm. Turning round, she saw Deira, and, eager to return to the sick room as she was, she felt that she must stop. "Deira, my dear, don't look like that. Grizel is alive; we hope she will soon be all right again."

"You don't understand," said Deira in husky tones. "It's my fault — if Grizel dies, I am a murderess! I did it!"

CHAPTER 9

The Feud Ends

"If Grizel dies, I am a murderess," repeated Deira tremblingly.

Miss Maynard looked at her keenly. She realized that the girl was on the verge of hysterics, so she pushed open the door of the study, and drew her in. "Now, Deira, sit down and tell me what you mean," she said quietly, as she closed the door and switched on the lights, for the sky had darkened ominously, and the little room was dusky.

"It was my fault," said Deira. "I was angry with Grizel. She threw a snowball at me, and it hit me. Sure, I thought 'twas on purpose she'd done it, and out of spite, so I picked up what was handy, and threw it. 'Deed, Miss Maynard, I never saw what it was. I didn't think at all! Oh, Miss Maynard, will she die?"

"Nonsense," said Miss Maynard briskly. "She's alive, and she may be ill; I can't tell you that she won't be. But we hope it won't be very bad. Only, Deira, think what your temper has done, and might have done. If Grizel had been killed you would never have forgiven yourself, I think. Now I must go. Mrs Russell may be wanting me." Deira nodded. She was putting a tremendous restraint on herself at the moment. Actually she wanted to scream and cry, she realized.

Miss Maynard knew what was passing in her mind, and guessed that, for the present, the girl was best left to herself. "You may stay here, Deira," she said gently. "I think you would rather do that than go back with the others. If anything happens with Grizel, you shall be told at once."

Then she left the room, and Deira, settling back in her chair, tried to recover herself.

The house was very silent now. The girls had gone to their form rooms, and were trying to fix their minds on their work. Mademoiselle had come over from Le Petit Chalet, and was giving the Fourth their lesson in French literature. The Sixth were working at maths by themselves, since Miss Maynard was still upstairs in the sick room. The Fifth were doing geography with Miss Wilson; and Miss Durrant was busy with the babies in their own house. As for the Third, Gertrud had come to them, and was giving them German *Dictat*. Outside, the snow had begun to drift again, and in the study the only sound was the crackling of the wood in the stove. The quiet soothed Deira. She got up from the chair, and moved over to the stove to feed it, and to warm herself. Now the excitement was gone, she felt cold.

She had been alone for more than an hour, when the door opened, and the Robin peeped in. "I want Tante Marguérite," she said.

"Madame is with Grizel," said Deira.

The Robin shut the door, and came up to her. "Is Grizel then sick?" she asked, lifting big dark eyes to the elder girl's face.

"She — is not well," stammered Deira. It was plain that the school baby knew nothing of what had happened. Could she tell her?

The Robin was full of sympathy. "*Pauvre* Grizel!" she said. "Has she eaten too much of chocolate?"

"She — has had — an accident. Madame and Miss Maynard are with her," said Deira.

"You are sorry 'cos you were cross with her? Never mind, *pauvre* Deira. She will soon be well," replied the Robin comfortingly. "Don't look so sad. Me, I will stay with you."

She slipped a chubby hand into Deira's, and snuggled up. The Irish girl sank on to the sofa, and lifted the baby on to her knee. The Robin put warm arms round her neck, and hugged her.

"Oh, but 'tis the darlin' you are!" murmured Deira, returning the hug. The Robin took it quite calmly as her due.

"How did Grizel hurt herself?" she asked suddenly, when she had bestowed a few more hugs on the elder girl.

Deira did not dare to tell her of what had happened. For

all she knew, it might be Mrs Russell's wish that the Juniors should know nothing of what had happened. So she temporized. "She got hit with a stone which was flung by mistake," she said, going as near the truth as she could.

"Oh!" The Robin drew in her breath in a long-drawn sigh. Then she turned and looked at Deira. "How dreadful!"

"It's awful!" said Deira unsteadily.

"An' it's dreadfuller for the one who threw the stone," went on the Robin, pondering things out in her baby way. She looked up, and caught sight of Deira's face. "Deira! was it *you*?"

There was a moment's silence. Then, "Yes," said Deira.

She half-expected the child to draw away in horror, but the Robin simply snuggled closer. "Oh, *pauvre* Deira!" she said, lapsing into the French.

Deira had heard the others say more than once that the Robin was the best comforter to have when you were in trouble, but she had never felt it before. Now, as the baby's arm encircled her neck, and the warm, soft weight tumbled into her lap, she felt the truth of it. "The stone — was — a mistake, Robin," she said unevenly. "I — I didn't know what it was!"

"'Course you didn't! Never mind, Deira. Tante Marguérite will understand — she always does! She'll know you're sorry, and she'll forgive you. So will Grizel. Don't cry, poor Deira!" For Deira had begun to cry, softly and bitterly, but in a very different way from what she had wished an hour ago. Unfortunately, once she had begun, she found it hard to stop; and when Mrs Russell, leaving Grizel for a few minutes to find the girl whom she had just been told was the cause of all the mischief, she found a Niobe-like scene, for by this time the Robin was crying too, out of sympathy for a grief she could feel, even if she couldn't understand it.

"Girls! Why are you crying like this?" asked the Head quietly. "Robin, you must stop at once."

The Robin had been trained to obedience, so she choked back her sobs and said brokenly, "Tante Guito, Deira is *so* sorry."

"I am sure she is," said Mrs Russell. "Crying won't help matters, though. So you must both stop at once, and you can run over to Le Petit Chalet, Robin. I will come to you at bedtime, but I can't come before. You will be good, *mein Vöglein*? — Yes, you may kiss Deira, and then run away. Joey shall come presently. Ask Gertrud to take you across — she is in the prefects' room. And be sure you are well wrapped up."

The Robin kissed Deira, and then trotted off to seek Gertrud, and give her Madame's message. Deira still sobbed on, though she was making heroic efforts to check her sobs.

The Head gave her a minute or two. Then she stooped over her. "Deira, I want you to control yourself. I cannot stay here long, for I must go back to Grizel. But I can't leave you like this. Come!"

Deira fumbled for her handkerchief, and the Head put her own into the hot hands. Then, while the girl dried her eyes, Madge Russell made up the fire in the stove again. When she thought that Deira had herself in hand, she spoke again. "Deira, Miss Maynard tells me that you say that you are to blame for what happened."

"Yes, Madame."

"I am very sorry for you, dear. And yet, I am glad in this. I think you will learn a very terrible lesson from this — how far your temper can take you when you give way to it. Will you try to think about it? I don't think you will ever again let yourself bear malice or carry on a feud with anyone as you have done this time. But remember that the girls are not to know if we can help it. It must lie between Grizel and yourself, and me. Miss Maynard knows, and I think we must tell Mademoiselle. But no one else is to learn it if we can manage it. Do you understand, dear?"

"The — the Robin knows," said Deira with a catch in her voice.

"Yes; but I shall tell her she is to say nothing. I am sorry she does know, but I suppose you couldn't help it. I don't believe, in the excitement of the moment, that they knew who threw the stone. I am going to ask you to be as much your usual self as possible. That will keep them from guessing. If they have missed you, they will only think that you were upset because you and Grizel had been on bad terms, and you were sorry you hadn't made it up. You are very tired now, so I am going to send you to bed. Go and undress yourself, and lie down. Try to sleep, and when you join the others, remember I have forbidden you to tell them anything."

Deira nodded and got up. She was worn out with the force of her emotions. She got to bed, and was there for the rest of the day. No one came near her, for they were still very anxious about Grizel, who had never recovered consciousness, but still lay in a state of coma. The others decided, as Mrs Russell had said, that Deira was upset by the thought that she had refused to make friends, and now she couldn't.

"Poor old thing! I bet she feels rotten!" said Jo Bettany to her own particular clan.

"I guess she's mad with herself all right," agreed Evadne Lannis, an American child famed in the school for her extensive slang vocabulary, which after three years was as unique as ever it had been, though she managed to curb her tongue a little during term-time. "I'd feel a skunk if I were her!"

"She must be very unhappy," sighed Frieda Mensch.

"Is — is Grizel going to *die*?" asked Simone in awed tones. The next minute she was sorry she had spoken, for Joey rounded on her with startling vehemence.

"For pity's sake, Simone, dry up! Of course she isn't! If you can't be more cheerful, just be quiet! You're a regular Job's comforter!"

What Simone might have replied to this tirade nobody ever knew, for just then Paula von Rothenfels announced that Dr Jem was coming up the path, and Jo darted out of the room to welcome him. She got little satisfaction, for Madge had been watching the path eagerly for the last hour, and was already in the passage, and sent her young sister back to the form room posthaste.

It was after seven that evening before the doctor left Grizel's bedside, and then he went to see Deira. Mrs Russell, however, came down to tell the anxious girls that it was all right. Grizel had come to herself, and had murmured something about a "rotten head" before she dropped off into natural sleep. She would be in bed for the next few days, but she would soon be herself again.

The girls were overjoyed at this news. It had seemed such a terrible thing that their jolly snow fight should have ended in this way. The older ones, at any rate, realized that there might have been a tragedy, though no one knew what had caused it. The general idea was that the ball which it was supposed had been flung at Grizel had got frozen — this was Joey's ingenious idea — and had been harder than the others.

The school went to bed that night happy once more, and Vanna even took the trouble to peep into Deira's cubicle to see if she were awake, so that she might hear the good news. Deira, however, was asleep, exhausted by repentance and excitement, so the Italian girl went on to her own domain, and the dormitory undressed in silence.

Grizel slept for most of the next two days, sleeping herself well again, as Dr Jem had prophesized. He went off to the Sonnalpe the next day, leaving his wife behind, for the path would be difficult, since the snow was still falling, and also she was anxious to see Grizel out of bed before she left her.

It was not till four days after the affair that Grizel asked anything about the other girls. Then, one afternoon, when Madge was sitting knitting by her side, she spoke. "Madame, will Deira come and see me, do you think?"

"I'll send her up after *Kaffee*," answered Mrs Russell, without any further comment. She had wondered how much Grizel knew of the accident, and if she was aware that the Irish girl was to blame for it. It was impossible to tell from the head girl's manner, but it looked rather like it. She had lain back on her pillows with a satisfied air, and said no more on the subject. Instead, she demanded to know when she might get up.

"I *loathe* bed!" she remarked. "It's all very well at the proper time, but I hate it when you've got to stay there!"

The Head laughed. "Bed in the early mornings is desirable, I suppose," she said.

"Rather! But I've had enough of it now. Can I get up tomorrow, Madame?"

"We'll wait till Dr Jem comes and sees you again," said Madge cautiously.

Grizel heaved a deep sigh, but the bell ringing for *Kaffee* precluded what she might have had to say, and Mrs Russell went off to join the others, leaving her in Matron's charge with a mischievous smile.

Five o'clock brought Deira to the room. A shame-faced Deira she was, with a scared look in her eyes, for she guessed that Grizel knew all there was to know about the accident.

Matron tucked some more wood into the stove, warned the visitor against exciting the invalid, and then went out, leaving them alone.

When she had gone Grizel held out her hand. "Will you shake now?" she asked.

Deira took it. "Do you know?" she said.

"Know what? About that stone? Yes; but you never meant it."

"I didn't," said Deira. "It was — temper. I'd have chucked a — a *log* at your head just then."

"Let's be thankful there wasn't one handy!" said Grizel with a grin. "Half a brick's good enough for me, thank you!" She gave Deira's hand a friendly grip.

"I'm sorry," said Deira.

"Righto! It was my fault as much as yours! I've a beastly tongue, and you've a beastly temper, so we'd better call it quits!"

Deira suddenly bent down and kissed Grizel. "You're jolly forgiving," she said, "'tis meself will remember that."

And so the feud was ended, and when Matron came half an hour later they were discussing the absolute awfulness of their last French translation.

CHAPTER 10

Marie's News

Marie von Eschenau went home for a weekend to be present at Wanda's betrothal party. That was the beginning of it all, as was proved later. Joey had been invited to go too, but she had started a cold. So she was relegated to the sick room while Marie went off with the aunt who came to bring her. It is a thirteen hours' run from Innsbruck to Vienna where Marie lived, so they had to start on the Thursday night, as the feast was on the Friday. Sunday would see her on the return journey, so that she might miss as little of school as possible.

"Lucky wench!" grumbled Joey when Marie came to say good bye and tell her how sorry she was that they couldn't both be there as they had hoped. "I say, you might bring me something from the show — a sprig of myrtle, or something."

"I will bring all I can," replied Marie, who was very fond of Joey in a quiet fashion, totally unlike Simone's rather hectic adoration. "I will also bring some cakes from that pastry-cook's you so much like."

"Marie, you *gem*! And some of those honey and nut things with cream in them! I love them!

"Also a large piece of Wanda's betrothal cake," added Marie. "I must go now, *Hertzliebchen. Auf Wiedersehen.*"

She went off, and Jo burrowed under her blankets and growled to herself about her ill-luck. Grizel, coming to sit with her later on, found her thoroughly disgruntled. Frieda had no better luck; and Simone left the room in tears!

On the Sunday Jo was pronounced to be all right again, and was allowed to join the rest of them in the house. There was to be no going out for her for another day or two. The snow had ceased, but it was freezing hard, and there was a bitter wind. As it was, she was too thankful to get away from the sick room and Matron, who was kind but dull, and be with all her friends again. So she made the best of things, though it was very tantalizing to see the pale winter sunshine turning the frozen snow into a thousand sparkling diamonds, and not go out in it. The Robin stayed with her while the others went for a long walk in the morning. When they had returned, Miss Durrant took the school baby for a brisk run to Seespitz, the tiny hamlet at the end of the lake.

As it was Sunday, the Juniors came over to the Chalet to spend the day as usual, and there was enough noise made to justify Miss Maynard's remarks about "monkey-houses". This was the one day in the week when the girls might speak their own language all the time without let or hindrance, and they made the most of it. French, German, and Italian were the chief languages, but there was English, of course, and some Norwegian, for there were four Norwegian girls in the school now; and a little Hungarian. As Miss Wilson had once said, when they all got started the Tower of Babel wasn't in it!

In the afternoon they passed the time in the usual way, and *Kaffee* was taken by themselves, the staff having a much-deserved rest over at Le Petit Chalet. The prefects were in charge, and Luise was in the kitchen with Rosa, the sister next in age to her — a treat always allowed the maid on Sundays.

After a while the talk turned on to the legends which surrounded the place. The Tyrol is full of stories, and Jo Bettany had learnt as many of them as possible, with an eye to the future, when she meant to use them in the books she was going to write. Frieda's father had been born and brought up by the Tiern See, and he had told the future novelist many tales, rejoicing in the deep interest she showed in them.

This afternoon, when they had finished their *Kaffee und Kuchen,* and had carried the china back to the kitchen as was the rule, the little ones insisted that Jo should tell them some of the stories.

"Tell how the Tiern See became a lake, Joey," pleaded

Margia Stevens's little sister Amy. "I love that story. I'm going to make a ballad of it some day."

Like Jo, Amy had resolved to be a writer when she grew up, but her bent was for verse, and she had written some very pretty things already. Their father was foreign correspondent to one of the big London dailies, and the two girls had lived in many places, leading a gypsy life till they had come to the school four years before this. Both were clever children, and their wandering years had given them a wide knowledge, as well as a fairly full vocabulary in more languages than little girls generally attain. Amy was a great favourite at school, so when she clamoured for the tale, the rest joined in, and Joey, nothing loth, began at once.

"Once upon a time," she said, dropping her voice to a mysterious undertone, "there was a great city where the lake now is. Its streets were thronged with citizens; beautiful houses rose on either hand; and in the centre was a magnificent church. Every weekday the streets rang with the cries of the merchants and pedlars; the clinking of the hammers on the beaten gold and silver work, which was the chief industry of the town; the shrill voices of chattering women, buying for the needs of their households; and the clatter of wooden shoes on the wide pavements. On Sundays the golden bells in the church steeple called folk to prayer, and the songs of sweet-voiced choristers rose to heaven from the heart of these mountains, where men lived in such wonderful surroundings. But the day came when the great prosperity of the people made them careless of what they owed to God. They forgot Him in their eager seeking after wealth and pleasure. Sunday by Sunday the bells called them to come to worship Him in vain, and things got to such a pass that the young lads used to play skittles in the aisles of the church even while divine service was going on, and the very priests themselves never said them nay.

"A good old hermit who lived near warned them that a judgment must fall on them as it did on Sodom and Gomorrah if they continued in their evil course, but they only mocked at him and paid no heed to his warnings. There came a Sunday when the sun shone down brightly on the city, with its ways thronged with people — men, women and children all going off on pleasure bent. Save for the priests who droned out the Mass so carelessly and badly that it was an insult to God, none had been near the church except the skittles-players. All seemed well, and they thought they had nothing to fear. Then, even while the streets rang with careless laughter, a terrible thing happened." Jo dropped her voice a full tone, and some of the little ones crept nearer together. "Water began to rise above the paving-stones of the church, and to wash about the feet of the false priests. The skittles were overthrown, and the players scattered in terror. But still the water kept on rising. It flowed out of the church now, and the houses were soon awash to the sills of the windows. Terrified, the people tried to flee, but there was no safety for them. The water rose and rose with appalling rapidity, and, ere the sun had sunk to his rest in the flaming west, there was no city left. Where it had been was a still blue lake, cradled amongst the mountains, and never more did anyone see the wicked people who had forgotten God in the days of their prosperity. Only on fine moonlight nights, when the summer stars are glowing in the skies, if you row across the Tiern See in a boat, you may see, if you look down through the water, the gilded spire of the church gleaming up from the depths; and if you listen, you may catch faintly the chime of its golden bells, rocked to and fro by the current."

Jo told the story well — it was one that appealed to her. When she had finished a deep sigh arose from the listening throng of girls, and there were cries for more. So she told them the story of the Bärenkopf mountain, which was rather similar, and which taught the same lesson; only, in this case, it was a wicked baron who was punished by the earth on which his castle was built being raised up so that castle, baron, and all were flung down into the valley, and some of the earth with them, till they were covered from sight.

It was very dark in the room, for someone had switched off the lights to give the tales more dramatic value, and the fire in the stove had sunk to a red glow, which made the shadows very big and fearsome. In their interest in Jo's narrative, no one noticed that the door had opened and shut again, and it came as a terrific shock to everyone when someone came across the room asking in astonished tones, "What do you do, then?"

Wild screams arose at the shock, and Gertrud made a mad dive to switch on the electric light. When they could see once more, Marie von Eschenau stood before them, her eyes like saucers with astonishment. Never had she been welcomed like this!

"Marie!" cried Margia, characteristically the first to recover herself; "when did you come?"

"Just now — with papa," replied Marie. "What is the matter with you all?"

"It's Jo's fault," returned Evadne. "She was telling us bogey-tales of round here, and we never heard you till we did."

Marie laughed at this Irish speech, and kissed Jo, who was standing looking rather pale. She had succeeded in frightening herself as well as her audience, and was slow to recover. "*Marie*?" she said. "I thought — I thought it was the wicked Baron Rheinhardt."

"Me, I thought it was the Devil," remarked Robin, who was still standing clutching Grizel, on whose lap she had been sitting.

"Well, it is me only," returned Marie. "Papa has to go to München, and he said that he would bring me with him today instead of waiting till tomorrow, as Tante Sofie does not wish to go home yet. Paula, I have here a box of bonbons for you from mamma, and some confitures from Tante Sofie." She held them out to her cousin, who took them rather dazedly. "Also, Wanda had two betrothal cakes, and I have one for us. It is outside in the car."

"Was it a decent show?" asked Jo, who was recovering from her shock rapidly now.

87

"But yes; it was very nice, and Wanda had on a new gown of white satin. There was a great feast and many speeches, and Wanda's *Brautigam* has sent chocolate for us all. I had a new frock, too — blue silk, and we were very merry. Wanda had many betrothal gifts, and she is very happy. They will be wedded in July, and Paula and I are to be her maids. Wanda wants as many of us to be there as possible. She and Friedel will come to see us next term."

Having scattered this information on them, she sat down by the stove and warmed her hands at the blaze which Grizel had just made. The others now came round her and poured out questions, demanding details.

"Wanda would be like a princess from Madame d'Aulnoy," murmured Simone sentimentally.

"Well, that's nothing fresh for her," said Jo amiably.

The rest agreed with her. Marie von Eschenau occupied the place of school beauty now, but everyone who had known her sister was agreed that Wanda far outdid the younger girl. She had passed into a sort of legend as far as the school was concerned. The picture of her in her white frock with her wreath of myrtle, and the string of pearls her uncle, the Graf von Rothenhels, Paula's father, had given her, was lovely enough to please the severest critic.

Herr Hauptmann Friedel von Glück came in for a very second share of the interest, though Marie had assured the girls that he was very amiable, and handsome as a prince out of the *Märchen*.

"Friedel's father is very kind," said Marie presently. "He asked many questions of me about us here, and says he thinks it is a very good school. Oh, and Joey, he knows all this part, for he used to climb the mountains round here when he was a boy, and he says he knows there are some wonderful caves nearby. He says you reach them through a narrow opening in the mountains, and you go down and down till you come to them, and they are all glittering inside as if they are made of diamonds. He thinks they must be under the lake, for he says they pass on to another cave, where there are stalactites, very beautiful. But no one knows about them, for people are afraid to venture, lest the water should break through.''

''I say! How interesting!'' Jo's fancy was caught at once. ''What else did he say about them, Marie?''

But the others were not very enthusiastic, and refused to listen to chatter about caves. What they wanted was to hear more of the betrothal feast. Herr Rittmeister von Eschenau came to say goodbye to his daughter before they were satisfied, and Marie had to stop her tale, to kiss him, and listen to his commands for good work and behaviour. Then he had to say a few words to Jo and Grizel, whom he knew quite well, and pat Maria Marani on the head. When he went out some of them went with him to rescue the spoils of the feast from the car, and then the bell for *Abendessen* rang, and after that the Juniors were packed off to bed, and the Middles had to follow half an hour later.

However, once they were undressed and in their pyjamas and dressing-gowns, Jo went through to Marie's cubicle, and, sitting on the bed with the *plumeau* tucked round her, proceeded to extract all that had been said about the caves. It was not much, but it was quite sufficient to excite Jo's imagination. ''I wonder where the opening is,'' she remarked, sitting with her knees hunched up, and her hair all on end as usual. ''Wouldn't it be exciting if some of *us* could find it? Just think! They might make a show place of it, and then they would need guides, and ever so many people would come, and the villagers would be able to make lots of money in the summer, so that they wouldn't be so poor!''

She spoke with fervour, for four years in the Tiern valley had taught her how pitiably poor the peasantry were. They had only the summer in which to garner their harvest. In the winter they had to live on their summer earnings, and often that meant hard living and being on the verge of starvation for most of them. In the mountainous regions the Tyrolese pray for a short winter, and a mild one. Otherwise, life is a bitter thing for them. In the summer most of the men are cowherds, taking the cows up to the pastures on the grassy alms which run like shelves along the lower slopes of the mountains, and live up there with them, many never coming down till the cows come down in the autumn. When winter comes they have to return to their homes in the villages, while the cattle are safely housed in sheds and byres, where one man can do the work that three or four do from May to September or thereabouts. They have no other means of livelihood, and in their homes tragedy stalks near during a long or hard season.

Jo knew this. She had come near it herself one year, when a poor family had been obliged to drown the pups of their great St Bernard, Zita, and had even spoken of shooting Zita herself. Joey had managed to rescue one of the puppies, and Madge had bought him for her. He was now a magnificent fellow, living up on the Sonnalpe, where he had more freedom than at school. The young headmistress had also taken care of Zita for the winter months, thus relieving the family of a heavy charge. After that, she had told them that if ever they were in such straits again, the big dog might winter at school. Since Zita's pups, when they arrived in the summer, were a source of income, the offer was gladly accepted and Zita had been at the school part of the previous winter. So far, she had not come this year, for the snow had come late, but if it continued for long the girls knew they might expect their great guest. Hence Jo's eagerness over the caves.

Marie, however, was a girl of very different kind. She was by no means adventurous, and rather shrank from the idea of going down into the bowels of the earth to hunt for caves. "I would rather not, Jo," she said. "But perhaps some of the men might go."

"Oh, but it would be gorgeous if our girls did it!" declared Joey. "It — it would be like saying 'thank you' for all they have done for us here."

"Well, I don't suppose we should be let," said Margia, who had strayed into the cubicle to listen to the conversation. "Think of the fuss they made when Grizel went off up the Tiernjoch, and that wasn't half so dangerous!"

"It was jolly dangerous," said Jo. "That beastly mist came down, and she was caught on that precipice! It was ghastly!"

"Well, I don't see us getting permission to go hunting for caves in the mountains," insisted Margia. "Madame would have a fit."

"She mightn't know till we'd found it."

"Don't be an ass! The very first thing they'd do if any of us went missing like that would be to ring them up at the Sonnalpe to see if we'd gone there!"

There was a good deal of truth in this, but what further Jo might have said on the subject was prevented by the ringing of the silence bell, and Miss Maynard came along five minutes later to switch their lights off.

CHAPTER 11

Half Term

The days passed quickly after this. Too quickly, Grizel thought, as she counted the weeks of school life left her, and felt how the time was going. She was devoted to her school, and she dreaded the break that the summer would bring. Always energetic, she devoted herself to doing all she could for the school, and, amongst other things, worked hard for the sale of work.

"I'm sick of fretsawing," grumbled Joey one Wednesday afternoon as she sat down to her treadle machine, and proceeded to adjust a fresh saw-blade. "As for the sale, I never want to hear of it again!"

"But there's so little time," said Grizel. "It will be half term in three days' time, and after that we shall be in the thick of it before we know where we are."

"Thank goodness it *is* half term!" said Jo vigorously. "And thank goodness the snow's stopped falling at last. Luise says that she thinks there will be no more now till the thaw. We always get a little then. I say, Grizel, d'you think we'll have a flood this year?"

"Shouldn't think so. Not since they deepened the bed of the stream again. We shall be safe enough. With that ditch round the place, I should think any flood there was would be drained off completely."

"You never know! Look at the Mississippi floods! They seem to get those every year, whatever they do."

"Oh, talk sense! This isn't the Mississippi, or anything like it! It's a different kind of soil, for one thing!"

Jo cut a piece of her new puzzle, and then sat back. "We aren't having any excitements this term. We generally have something thrilling at least once in the term. I don't count your accident, 'cos it didn't affect all of us, except that we all had fits about you. I mean like the flood we had two years

92

ago. Or the fire last summer term, when the fireball dropped during the thunder storm. *That's* what I call an excitement!''

"I dare say you do!" retorted Grizel. "Personally, I prefer a quiet life. There's the sale at the end of term if you want any excitement. And we are going up to the Sonnalpe for half term. You be contented with that, and get on with your puzzles. I want twenty, if you can manage them.''

"I've got nine done," said Jo. "This is the tenth. I don't believe you'll sell more than fifteen, anyway, even if I can get them done. I wish Friday was here.''

"It'll come jolly soon. You'd better wish for decent weather while you *are* about it! I know that it's unlikely to snow again, but if a howling wind gets up, we shan't be allowed to go. That path is fairly well exposed to a west wind, and it's not too nice in a north gale.''

"Oh, the wind's going to stay put," declared Jo. "It *couldn't* be so maddening as to rise when we want it to be calm!''

"The wind never does do what you want," said Grizel. "I say, Joey, *do* get on. It will be time for singing soon, and you could get a lot done now if you choose.''

Joey grunted, but made her treadle go as fast as she could, cutting the puzzle carefully, but at such a speed that it was small wonder that her saw suddenly broke off. "That settles it! I'm not going to fuss to stick another in!" she announced. "Plato's arrived already, and the bell will go in a minute. I've cut a third of this beastly thing, and I've only three saws left. Someone going to Innsbruck on Saturday will have to fetch me some more.''

"I will buy them, Joey," said Frieda.

"Thanks awfully. I'm going to give it a rest till after the exeat. There's the bell!''

She finished putting her work away, and then dashed off to the singing class, where Mr Denny — Plato, to the girls — proceeded to be more eccentric than usual. He always spoke in the language of Tudor times, and, since his one idea was his art, he made many startling statements. From his point of view, all education should be based on music, and he quoted from Plato's *Republic* in season and out — hence his name. The rest of the week was full of hard work, though Jo obstinately refused to touch her fretwork again, in spite of all Grizel could say!

It was a beautiful day, with a nip of frost in the air, just enough to make brisk walking enjoyable, and the climb up to the Sonnalpe a real treat. The Robin was to be carried up the path on her father's back — he having come over to Briesau to fetch the three girls — and the others would scramble and climb as best they could. They started off about eleven o'clock, for it would take them four hours, and the daylight would be fading by two, since the mountains cut it off.

Well wrapped up, they tramped down to the lakeside, and there Captain Humphries strapped on their skates for them, and they set off across the frozen lake. They were all expert skaters now, even the Robin managing well on her small blades, and they were soon at Seespitz, the nearest point to the foot of the Sonnenscheinspitze, the mountain of the Sonnalpe. There they took off their skates and left them with Frau Hamel, mother of two of the girls, Sophie and Gretel, who were still in school, before they set off along the narrow path till they came to the foot of the mountain.

"Gorgeous day!" said Joey, stopping to sniff the fresh, bracing air. "I do love a sharp, clear day like this! Think what it'll be like in England now!"

Captain Humphries smiled as he lifted the Robin, preparatory to beginning the climb. "I have not been in England for a good many years now, but I can imagine it!"

"Wet — cold — *slushy*!" said Jo, with a pause between each of the words. "I love England, of course, but oh, I loathe her winters!"

"Me, I do not like them at all," said the Robin from her perch on her father's shoulder. "I like the Tiern See, though, and I *love* going to see Tante Marguérite!"

"We all do," said Grizel, as she struggled up the

94

rocky path. "Come on, Jo! Don't lag behind!"

"It's so slippery," complained Joey as she scrambled breathlessly after the others.

"Never mind; we shall soon be there," said the captain, who was swinging over the ground as if he had no burden at all. Then he set his little girl down, and went back to help the older girls.

It took three hours' hard scrambling to bring them to the easier path which led finally to the Sonnalpe, and the sun had disappeared by that time. Joey stood and looked down at the valley below. The lake was black with its ice, and the snow lay white all round it. Immediately beneath them was Seespitz, with its Gasthaus and villas. Farther along was Buchau, where there were two or three farmhouses, and the ferry-landing. Beyond lay the pine woods, black against the snow, and beyond them the great limestone crags and peaks of the mountains.

In the west the sun was sinking in a glory of saffron light, which told of high winds for the morrow, but Jo paid no heed to this at the moment. She stood there, her little pointed face glowing with the beauty of it all, her black eyes soft and unfathomable.

"Come on!" said matter-of-fact Grizel at last when her patience was worn out. "It's after three, and we've got half an hour's walk yet before we reach the Sonnalpe."

With a deep sigh Jo turned her back on the glory, and they set off on the last part of the way. It was very easy now, so the Robin was walking, her hand in her father's, her tongue going at a great rate. Jo and Grizel came behind them, arm in arm, for the path was fairly broad hereabouts, and saying little. Jo was still entranced by the memory of the loveliness she had witnessed, and Grizel was tired and out of breath. They reached the alpe itself at last, and here they found Dr Jem waiting for them. "Hullo!" he said. "I saw you people from the sanatorium, so I waited for you. I've got the run-about here, so I'll take you all along to Die Blumen in it. Come along! You'll be at home in ten minutes or less now!"

"Thank goodness!" sighed Grizel as she fell into step between them. "I'm pumped!"

"You're like Hamlet, my child — fat and scant of breath," he said teasingly.

"I'm *not* fat!" returned Grizel indignantly. "I'm out of training, if you like. We've had no chance of it this term with such awful weather. But fat I am *not*!"

"You ass, Grizel!" said Joey. "You always rise to Jem. I can't think why you do it!"

Grizel laughed, her momentary indignation forgotten as they rounded a curve and saw the doctor's little runabout standing before the steps that led up to the great sanatorium. "Well, I'm tired, anyway! I'm jolly glad you saw us and waited, Dr Jem!"

"You're late, aren't you?" he said. "I know Madge expected you earlier than this!"

"It was such a pull up," explained Joey. "It's beastly slippery too."

"We're here now, anyway, and that's all that matters," laughed Grizel as she slipped into her seat and held out her arms for the Robin. "Can you squeeze in, Jo?"

"Rather! How's Uncle Ted going to manage though?"

"I'm going to walk," said the captain. "I have a call to make at Wald Villa before I come up to Die Blumen. Tell Mrs Russell I'll be along presently, will you?"

"Very well," said the doctor. "All safe, you people? All right! So long, Humphries!" He pressed the starter, and they were off and bowling jerkily over the snowy ground.

"I don't think much of your roads," chuckled Joey. "A bit on the bumpy side, aren't they?"

"A bit," agreed the doctor. "We are going to have them seen to during the spring. Here we are! Tumble out, and run along in. Madge will be waiting for you."

They scrambled out and ran up the long path which led to the door, where Madge, wrapped in a shawl, was waiting to welcome them. In the summer the ground on either side would be a beautiful flower garden; but now it was white and bare, with a few miserable-looking bushes here and there. They raced to the door where their hostess was standing, and were all caught in a clump as she pulled them in. "How late you people are! I was beginning to think something had happened and you weren't coming! Come along in! Straight upstairs, and get your things off and change your shoes! You know your rooms, don't you? Joey's next to ours, and Grizel on the other side of her. Robin, you are to sleep in papa's dressing room, just opposite. See to her, Joey; I'm busy cooking."

Joey nodded, and they ran upstairs and along the passage till they came to their rooms. They were very dainty, furnished in the fashion of the country, with panelled walls and high white-washed ceilings. The beds had white, tent-like curtains, and one or two copies of famous pictures hung on the walls. Jo's room communicated with her sister's, and the Robin's with her father's. None of them had brought any clothes, for they kept some there in case of need. They got out of their outdoor things, changed their sturdy boots and stockings for silk and dancing sandals, brushed their hair — a very necessary thing in Joey's case — and finally ran downstairs again.

"I am hungry," observed the Robin.

"Are you, dearie? Well, Marie is bringing *Kaffee und Kuchen* now, so you won't be hungry long," replied Madge, lifting the small girl on to her knee.

"That's a mercy!" declared Joey. "I'd have had to tighten my girdle or something if you had wanted us to wait much longer. Here's Jem again. I say, Jem, I've nearly finished my story! The only thing I can't decide is what to do about marrying them."

"Aren't you going to marry them?" asked Madge, who had been privileged to read the first part of this tale. "I think I should, Joey. What else can you do with them?"

"I could kill 'Raymonde' off," said Jo. "Then 'Adelaide' could — could—"

"Well? Could — what?" demanded Jem.

"Go into a convent?" suggested Grizel.

"Of course not, idiot! She's not a Catholic!"

"Marry them, of course," said Madge. "Don't make them unhappy, Jo! Even if it's only a story, let them end up all right."

"Lots of stories don't," argued Jo as well as she could for a mouthful of cake. "Look at *A Tale of Two Cities*, and *The Old Curiosity Shop*, and *The Mill on the Floss*."

"It requires genius to write a tragedy, Jo," said her brother-in-law. "I grant you that Dickens and George Eliot got away with it; but nothing is worse than the mawkish rot that some people write."

"Well, there's *Comin' through the Rye*, an' *Trilby*."

"I've never read the first, but Du Maurier was as much a genius as Dickens," said Jem.

Jo had just remembered that Madge would know nothing about the caves, and she promptly poured out all she had gleaned from Marie, together with her own theories on the subject. The doctor was interested at once. "I say, that's interesting!" he said. "When I was last in Vienna I met that open-air fiend, Professor von der Witt — you remember, Madge? He said he thought there ought to be something of the kind hereabouts, but I don't think he knew anything definitely. I must write and let him know about this!"

A ring at the telephone put a stop to their chatter just then, and Jem went to answer it. He came back looking serious. "It's the sanatorium. That poor fellow is worse again — Maynard thinks he can't last many hours now. I must go, dear."

Madge rose at once. Seven months as a doctor's wife had taught her many things. Her face was very grave as she followed her husband from the room. The girls looked at each other miserably.

Only the Robin seemed untouched. "Papa, is it someone going to Paradise?" she asked.

"Yes, my pet," he replied quietly.

"Let's go and see Rufus," suggested Grizel, shying away from the subject. "He's in the shed, Captain Humphries, isn't he?"

"Yes," said the captain. "Go through the kitchen, children, and don't stay long. Perhaps you had better go and bring him here."

They went off to call Joey's best-loved possession, a magnificent specimen of a magnificent breed, and presently returned with him, just as Madge entered. The Robin's father had gone, but she joined in the romping of the others. Six o'clock brought the baby's bedtime, and she was whisked off, Rufus following, to have her bath, while the elder girls settled themselves with books.

There was a long silence in the pretty room, then Jo put her book down. "Grizel!"

"Yes?"

"Grizel, isn't it awful? Just when we are having a jolly time, that poor man over there is — dying."

Grizel nodded. She was older than Jo, but she had not thought as deeply as the younger girl. Her mind had been running on the same subject while she had been pretending to be buried in her book. She had neither the Robin's baby faith, nor Jo's contemplative nature, and she shied away from her thoughts. "You'd better go on with your book," she said. "It's nearly time for *Abendessen*."

Jo returned to the pages, but she was not following them. Her thoughts were all on that mysterious thing that was happening at the sanatorium.

Madge divined it as soon as she entered the room after tucking up the Robin, and she crossed over to her sister. "Joey, you need not be sorry for this poor fellow. He will be joining those he loved best tonight. The priest was here this morning, and he is prepared."

The two girls came and sat on the floor beside her.

"Madame, what is death?" asked Grizel.

"Just falling asleep with God — to awake in His presence — that's all," said Madge Russell.

99

"Then why are we afraid of it?"

"Because it means a change, and most of us are afraid of changes that we don't understand. But, Grizel, there is nothing to fear, really, any more than there is anything to fear when we fall asleep at night."

Grizel sat silent, thinking this over.

"God is with us through it all?" asked Joey.

"Yes, Jo. He never leaves us if we have faith in Him."

It was not many weeks later that this came back to both girls in another and very different place, and those quiet sentences helped them to face what looked like certain death with courage and calm.

Now, as they sat there, the telephone bell shrilled. Madge rose and answered it.

Presently she came back. The two faces turned to her with questioning in their eyes.

She nodded. "Yes; he has fallen asleep, and will waken in Paradise."

They said no more, but the rest of the evening was a quiet one. Their weekend had begun sadly, but, somehow, they were not as sad as they had thought they would be, and the event cast no gloom over their holiday.

Jem had not returned by nine o'clock, when Madge insisted on Joey and Grizel going to bed, since they were tired from their scramble.

"I'd like to go on with my book," Joey protested.

"You may do that tomorrow," said her sister serenely. "Bedtime for you now. Your eyes are like saucers, and Grizel's aren't much better. Off you go, both of you! I'll come round and put the lights out presently."

Grizel was already asleep when she went to them, but Joey was lying awake. "That's all it is?" she asked, apropos of nothing, as her sister bent to kiss her.

Madge understood. "Yes, Jo; that's all."

"I shan't forget," said Joey. "O-o-ow! How tired I am. G'night, Madge!"

CHAPTER 12

The Robin Is Lost

"Girls, have you seen the Robin?"

The prefects looked up as Miss Maynard came into their room, this question on her lips.

"But no, Madame," said Vanna. "I have not seen her all day."

"Nor I," added Rosalie. "When did anyone last see her?"

"Nobody seems to know," replied the mistress with a worried look. "Amy says she went off for her afternoon nap as usual, and Klara saw she was tucked up. Since then, no one knows anything about her."

"Is she with Joey?" asked Grizel.

"Jo has been working all the afternoon, and knows nothing about her. She was never missed till half an hour ago. Girls, are you *sure* you haven't seen her anywhere?"

They shook their heads.

"We had German literature at two," said Grizel, "and at three we came up here. I had my lesson with Herr Anserl at half past, but I saw nothing of her then."

"Well it's very mysterious," said Miss Maynard. "Where *can* she have got to?"

"Could she have gone to talk to Luise?" suggested Gertrud. "She is very fond of her, and Luise loves our baby."

"That's an idea. She may be in the kitchen."

"I'll run down and see, shall I?" proposed Mary, getting to her feet. "I won't be a second, Miss Maynard."

She tore off downstairs, but returned to say that Luise had seen nothing of the Robin that day. "And please, Miss Maynard, she thinks she may be in the shed with Rufus."

Rufus had come back from the Sonnalpe with his mistress, who had declared that she simply *must* have him with her

101

for the rest of the term. As there were only five weeks left, Madge had agreed, and the big dog had been duly installed in the shed when the girls came down with him. Miss Maynard promptly went off to see if she could find Robin there, and the prefects returned to their various pursuits without thinking any more about it. It was something of a shock to them, therefore, when the mistress returned ten minutes later to say that only Joey was with the big dog, and she had declared that the Robin had not been there when she had come.

The Seniors dropped their work, and at once Grizel began an organized search party, and sent them over to Le Petit Chalet, forming another with which she hunted through the chalet till there was not a hole nor a corner which they had not investigated. It was in vain. The Robin had vanished.

"It's as strange as it was the day that you and Eigen rescued Rufus, Joey," said Simone, referring to one of Jo's exploits of two years before; "we couldn't find you then, and we can't find the Robin now."

At the reminder, Jo had rushed out of the room.

"Where has she gone?" demanded Marie von Eschenau.

They were answered by the return of Jo, leading Rufus, and Grizel behind her.

"Rufus can track her!" cried his owner. "He helped me to find Elisaveta in the summer, and this is snowtime. St Bernards are always able to do things in the snow! Hang on to him, someone, while Grizel and I get our coats and tammies!"

Evadne obligingly caught the dog's harness — and the pair vanished, to reappear wearing their outdoor things, while Grizel had the Robin's rolled up into a bundle under her arm. Jo was waving a vacuum flask which Luise had filled with hot coffee, and they looked well equipped for their expedition.

There was no staff to stop them, for all the staff were busy hunting through the grounds in case the little girl had got lost there. Grizel gave her orders. "Gertrud, go over and tell Klara to have the Robin's bed warmed for her. Rosalie, see that there is a hot bath ready. Vanna and Luiga, you might go and look after the babies. Deira, you and Mary must see to the Middles. Eva, go and tell Mademoiselle that we have gone with Rufus to see if he can track her. Ask Matey to ring up the Sonnalpe, and ask if Doctor Jem can come down *without alarming Madame*! The rest of you, for any sake, be good! There's enough trouble as it is. Come on, Jo!"

They dashed off, and presently the girls saw them at the gate of the fence, showing the dog something small, which Evadne pronounced to be one of the Robin's gloves.

Evidently Rufus found the scent at once, for he dashed forward at a pace that made the girls pant breathlessly after him. Jo had hold of his chain, but he towed her along, Grizel running hard to keep up with them. Right round the fence he led them, and up to the pine woods that covered the slopes of the Bärenbad Alpe. There he began to lead them through the trees, keeping far from the path which they usually followed.

"Help!" thought Grizel. "How on earth has she got this far?"

On went Rufus, never slackening his pace for a moment, and on went the girls. They were now reaching a part of the mountain that they did not know. How the Robin's baby feet had carried their owner this distance was a question neither Grizel nor Jo could settle.

Just as both of them were beginning to feel that they could not go on any longer, and Joey was starting a stitch in her side, the dog suddenly stopped, circled round restlessly once or twice, and then, sitting down on his haunches, threw up his nose and bayed loudly. The melancholy sound nearly finished Jo, who was tired, and Grizel felt suddenly helpless and despairing. "What *has* happened to her," cried the head girl. "Oh, Rufus, do stop that awful noise. Make him dry up, Joey!"

Joey put her arms round his neck, and kissed him on his cold nose. Then she turned to Grizel. "Grizel, where has she gone to? Do you think Rufus means that she's buried in the snow?"

"Nonsense! How could she? It's as hard as iron!" Grizel stamped on the ground to give emphasis to her words, and the ringing sound of her nail-studded boots on the frozen snow gave point to her rejoinder.

"Then what has happened?"

"Someone may have found her, and carried her," suggested Grizel.

"But who?"

"That's more than I can tell you. I didn't think anyone came here. It's supposed to be haunted, you know. Look here, Jo, suppose we go on a little farther and try him again. He might be able to pick up the scent. I don't think she's been carried off, if that's what you are thinking. There's no one — *what's that*?"

Jo turned, and looked fearfully in the direction in which she was pointing. What she expected to see, neither she nor anyone else could have told at the moment. What she actually did see was a deep cleft in the rock wall not far from where they were standing, and asleep in it was a strange old man with long white beard and hair, and in his arms, warmly wrapped up in an old deerskin, was the Robin. Both recognized her black curls at once, and both made for the group immediately. Rufus followed them, barking vociferously.

The noise woke the strange bedfellows, and the Robin sat up, holding out her arms to the girls, while the man lay where he was, gazing at them with wild blue eyes in which there was something which Grizel mentally described as "uncanny".

"*Herzliebchen*!" Jo had caught the baby to her. "Little beloved! How could you run away like this and leave us? Are you cold, *Bübchen*?"

"But no, Joey, I am very warm," replied the Robin,

rubbing her curls well into Jo's mouth as she snuggled up to her. "This gentleman, Herr Arnolfi he is, and he has kept me so warm. He was taking me to see where the fairies live, and we got tired, so we sat down to rest."

Grizel turned to the old man, seeing that Joey was too busy hugging the fond lamb to trouble with him. "Why did you take her off?" she demanded in German.

He chuckled in a meaningless manner, rising slowly to his feet. "It is the queen of the fairies, my little lady. I was but taking her back to her own realms."

With a little gasp of horror Grizel realized that they were dealing with a madman. He might be harmless, but none the less he was insane. If he chose to resist them they were only two girls, and she had read stories which told her of the strength of insanity. Somehow they must get the baby home without frightening her. Choosing her words carefully, she answered, "It is the wrong time of year, Herr Arnolfi. Now, the fairies are all asleep till the spring shall come. Then she may go back, but now, she would be alone without attendants to wait on her. You would not be so cruel as to condemn a queen to that, would you?"

He looked at her, a madman's cunning in his eyes, that wandered restlessly over them. "How do I know that you mortals will let her go? I am of the fairy-folk myself. Give me the little queen, and I will be her faithful attendant until the spring shall come."

"But it is not fitting that she should go thus," persisted Grizel, all her wits bent on getting them away before his insane anger should break out. "She is not robed as befits a queen. Neither has she jewels." In English she added, "Joey! Get her wrapped up, and away! Put her on Rufus's back."

Jo at once lifted the child on to the back of the great dog, who was well able to take the light weight, and had often acted the part of horse before. But she made no attempt to move. She had grasped what was the matter, and she had no intention of leaving Grizel to face the maniac by herself.

The Robin, not realizing, simply took the dog's fur in her hands, prepared for a merry ride on his back.

"Get off with her," said Grizel urgently. "*Quick*, Joey!"

"And leave you to this lunatic? It's likely, isn't it?" remarked Jo scornfully.

"Then tie her on, and send Rufus home. He can carry her easily. But get her away!"

Joey obeyed promptly, tying the Robin as well as she could with gym girdle and scarf. "Hold tight, darling," she murmured. "Tell them to let Rufus bring them here when you get home."

The lunatic had watched their movements with increasing suspicion. Now he turned to Grizel. "The queen has her steed. But you must go. It is not fitting that mortals should behold the court of the fairies. Go, I tell you! Go!"

He was plainly becoming excited. Grizel nodded to Jo, who guessed what it meant. Flinging out her arm in the direction in which they had come, the younger girl cried, "Home, Rufus! Home, boy!"

The gallant animal at once set off, loping along easily. As he sped off the madman gave vent to such an unearthly yell as terrified the two girls left behind, and he made off after the great dog, tearing over the snow with gigantic bounds, that, it seemed, must bring him up to Rufus in no time. But Rufus was alarmed, and he quickened his pace, the Robin clinging with terrified grip to him.

"Come on, Jo!" shrieked Grizel, catching Joey's hand. "*Run*!"

They set off at their best pace, running down the slope away from the cleft. The lunatic was still pursuing Rufus and his precious burden, but even his insane strength was running out, and already he was losing ground. Grizel realized that as soon as he saw this he would probably make for them, to wreak his vengeance on them, and she made no attempt to follow the dog's tracks. Instead, she ran steadily out from them, trusting that the shape of the valley would bring them to some well-known path sooner or later. As for

Jo, she couldn't even think. She simply ran blindly on, clinging to Grizel in a blind faith which was their salvation, for had she known that they were not following Rufus, the chances are that she would have argued the point. As it was they tore on, breathless, terrified, and well-nigh blind with fear. Finally, Jo tripped up over a buried tree trunk and fell headlong, dragging Grizel after her.

They were up in a moment and dashing on with bursting lungs, but the fall had broken their headlong flight, and in less than three minutes they knew that they could not go on. Their run fell to a walk, and, finally, Joey sank down on the ground, her hand at her side where the cruel stitch was catching, and fighting for breath. Grizel was not in a much better state, but she was able to realize that they must not stay there. The cold was cruel, and already the stars were beginning to show in the skies, and they had no means as yet of knowing where they were.

The head girl bent and pulled Jo to her feet. "Come on, Joey! We can't stop here. Hang on to me, and I'll haul you along."

"I can't!" gasped Jo. "Grizel, I can't! Let me alone! Let me alone!"

But Grizel persisted. In spite of her own weariness she managed to drag Jo along with her, though it was a slow progress, and she was terrified in case they were going round in a circle, and should come up with the old madman again. Joey was becoming a dead weight and was ceasing to protest against being made to walk. Grizel knew that she herself could not go on much longer, and she shuddered inwardly as she thought of what might happen if they had to go much farther.

Mercifully, help was nearer at hand that she had supposed. Just as she was beginning to decide that she could not move another foot, the sound of voices came to them from amongst the trees, and there were lights to be seen moving in their direction. With a final effort the head girl let go her hold of Joey and called as loudly as she could. Then she, too, sank down on the ground, utterly exhausted. Three men who had come over the great Tiern Pass from Germany found them there two minutes later, and had to carry them to Lauterbach, the little hamlet at the Austrian end of the pass. Neither of them recovered consciousness till they were safely in one of the chalets, where the rescuers dosed them with brandy, to bring them to. It was some time before they could recover their wits sufficiently to say where they came from, and by that time the Chalet people, led by Dr Jem and Rufus, had succeeded in tracking them to the hamlet.

Both were so completely done that they had to stay where they were for the night, and when they were brought home next day they were put straight to bed and kept there. Joey was in the worse state. Grizel was as strong as a young pony, and, except for a stiffness which soon wore off, she recovered from her fright and exertion rapidly.

Jo, on the other hand, was so worn out that it was decided to separate her from everyone, and she was taken to her sister's bedroom, where she stayed for ten days, finally coming downstairs looking white and big-eyed, and inclined to be easily upset. Of the three the Robin came off best. She had been frightened by the old man's chasing of her and Rufus, but they had soon got away from him, and they had not gone far before meeting the search party from the Chalet, which had set out as soon as Eva had given Mademoiselle Grizel's message. It had been by accident that they had gone in that direction at all, but the baby was quickly taken from her perch and carried home in Miss Durrant's arms.

Her story, when they got it from her, was that she had finished her afternoon nap, and had got up, dressed herself, and gone out into the playing field, as she was permitted to do on fine days. She had been running along by the fence when the old man had suddenly appeared at the other side, and had called to her and told her to come with him, for he would take her to Fairyland. She had never thought of its being naughty, but had gone off quite happily, and he had been very good to her. When she had grown tired he had offered to carry her, but she had refused, for she wanted to be a real schoolgirl, and she was a Brownie, anyway, and Brownies don't fuss over trifles. At last, when they had reached the cleft, he had picked her up, and told her that now he was going to take her through it to Fairyland, where she would be queen. Only he was tired and must rest. So he had sat down and taken her in his arms.

The next thing she knew, Joey and Grizel and Rufus were there, and then they had put her on Rufus's back, and sent him home with her, and the old man had been *very* angry. He had run after them, but Rufus had run faster, and then Miss Maynard and Miss Durrant and Miss Wilson had come, and Miss Durrant had carried her home. And she was sorry. Please would they forgive her?

"You were very naughty, my child," said Mademoiselle. "You are not permitted to leave the school by yourself. Poor Joey and Grizel had a terrible time, and now they are ill in bed because you were so naughty."

The Robin wept bitterly. She adored Joey, who was her ideal in everything, and she was not allowed to go near her beloved. Grizel, too, had been very kind to her. They could have inflicted no worse punishment on her than she had brought on herself, and after a little more talk Mademoiselle consented to forgive her, and kissed her.

However, that escapade of the Robin's was to have much farther reaching results than they yet realized, but after Grizel had been gently told that she should never have gone off as she did, nothing more was said. In Jo's case, scolding had to be put on one side. Her nerves had received a severe shock, and she was not herself all the rest of the term.

As for the old man, he had vanished as completely as if he had never existed. If it had not been that all three girls told the same story, and told it independently, those in authority would have decided that he had been a figment of imagination.

The Briesau people had another explanation of him. *They* said that he was a devil who had vanished by the aid of Satan, and that the children had had a narrow escape from being carried off to hell!

CHAPTER 13

The Holidays

The rest of that term passed quietly and quickly. The girls busied themselves with their preparations for the sale, and Joey managed to content herself with her fretwork. She remained very quiet, and was still easily upset, even when the end of term came, so that the staff were thankful that in a few days she would be safely in her sister's care.

Rufus, who had proved himself such a hero, was well on the way to being spoiled, for everyone petted him, and he was rewarded with tit-bits dear to his doggish heart, and some of the Middles nearly came to blows over the question of who was to look after him while his mistress was absent from him. It was finally settled by the prefects themselves, who undertook to see to his grooming and baths, and so saved the school from what looked like some promising feuds.

"For goodness' sake, try to behave as though you *were* Middles, and not Juniors!" said Grizel, whose first act on leaving the sick-room had been the settlement of this affair. "*None* of you will have anything to do with him, because *we* will do all he needs."

The sale was a huge success. By the time the girls had laid out all they had made themselves, and added to it all the contributions from other people, they found that they had enough for two needlework stalls, one handiwork stall, a sweet stall, a toy stall, and the little ones' lucky dip. When it was all over they counted their takings, and there was wild rejoicing when they found that they had made enough to keep one of the free beds filled for a whole year.

"I vote we do this every year," said Grizel, as she locked her cash-box, "then it could be the Chalet School bed, and Doctor Jem would always feel sure of *that*, anyway."

"Good idea," said Mary. "I vote we do. What do you others think?"

They all agreed, and Grizel was made to sit down then and there to write to Doctor Jem, telling him what they intended doing.

The result of this was that when Grizel, Joey, and the Robin put in an appearance at the Sonnalpe on the first day of their holidays, they were escorted ceremoniously to the sanatorium, and taken to the big free ward for children. There were no patients there yet, though some would be arriving shortly. It was a sunny room, with picture-flowers, and a glorious view from the windows. But the girls paid no heed to all this. One thing only caught their eyes. The middle cot had a brass plate over it, and on this was engraved "The Chalet School Bed".

"Jem! You *ripper*!" gasped Jo. "Oh, how decent of you to get it done before we came up!"

"It's wonderful!" said Grizel. "Ever so nice, Doctor Jem."

"I like the shiny thing," remarked the Robin gravely. "Why has it our name up, Oncle Jem?"

They explained it to her carefully, and she listened with a beaming face. When they had finished, she heaved a deep sigh. "I will save all my *Schillings*," she said.

Doctor Jem stooped and kissed her. "You are a darling," he said.

The Robin kissed him back, and then turned to Mrs Russell. "Will it please you, Tante Guito?"

"Very much, my pet."

The next few days were spent in taking walks in the neighbourhood, but they soon exhausted all the possibilities, and by the time they had climbed the mountain twice they were ready for something fresh.

"That's the only drawback to here," said Grizel, as they sat in the salon after *Kaffee* one day. "There aren't many places you can go to, and now it's thawing, the whole place is ankle-deep in mud! This is the second time today I've had to change my stockings!"

"Well, I had to change every solitary thing," declared

Jo between two bites of *apfeltorte*. "You'll have fits when you see my laundry, Madge!"

Madge Russell laughed. "I don't doubt it for one moment. If there *is* any mud you can get into, you seem to make for it headlong, Jo. I never knew anyone like you for it! You're worse than Dick used to be!"

"Has the Indian mail come today?" asked Jem.

"Yes; but I haven't opened it yet. It's a thick package this time, so I expect Mollie managed to get time to put in a decent letter for once," said his wife, as she produced the letter from her twin brother, who was in the forest service in the Dekkan. "Yes; there's something from her."

"Goodness! What a screed!" ejaculated Jo. "Read us what she says, Madge."

Madge nodded and began:

DEAR PEOPLE, — It is such ages since I wrote you a decent letter, that I thought I'd take this opportunity, while mother is with us and looking after the twins and baby, to let you know what we are doing. I should say, what we are going to do, I suppose. Because this is to warn you that we are coming home in June, and hope to be with you in August. Dick gets leave early in May, and it's a six months' furlough this time. We are coming straight to you, so I hope you can have us. If you can't, we'll go to one of the hotels by the lakeside.

If you're not all dying to see your nephew and nieces, you ought to be! Rix and Peggy are imps of wickedness. Where they get it from I can't imagine! Not from me, that's certain. I suppose it must be Jo, for Dick says you were never as sinful as our twins are. As for Babs, she's still at the stage when she sleeps most of the time, and is a good little thing. She is like Dick — the image of him, I think! He, of course, says he doesn't know where I see it. The first time I told him he had the cheek to go off to the nearest mirror and examine himself carefully, murmuring all the time, "I *may* be plain, but I'm not as bad as all that!" As I told him, he doesn't deserve a daughter at all!

Rix is like that photo of Madge she sent us on her wedding-day. Peggy is dark like me, and Dick says, like Joey too. Can you picture them, *my* children? Dick and me with three kiddies. Of course, Babs is only three weeks old yet, but still it does make us seem *old*! After all, the twins are thirteen months now; they can walk and talk, though a lot of their conversation is absolutely unintelligible.

Babs is to be christened next Sunday. We are going to call her Mary — after me; and Bridget after my little sister, who died before I was born. I suppose she will be Biddy as soon as she is old enough for a name. That won't be for ages yet.

What is happening at school? Have you had any more excitements this term? I am longing to see it, and to get to know all the girls. You've written so much about them that I feel as if I knew them all. We want to stay till term begins again — I suppose you'll have broken up by the time we arrive? Still, I shall hope to see the Robin and Juliet and Grizel, if she hasn't left you by then.

Babs is howling for me, so ayah will be fetching her. Therefore, my dear relations, I must wind up this epistle. You can't say I haven't done you proud this time! — Much love to all, from   MOLLIE.

"Isn't she a sport?" said Jo enthusiastically. "Fancy me with three nieces and nephews!"

"You've only one nephew and two nieces," Grizel pointed out to her.

"Oh, well, you know what I mean. What does Dick say, Madge?"

"Mainly full of his furlough," replied her sister. "I'm glad they're coming. I've been wanting to know Mollie ever since I first heard of her. From her letters, she's a dear. Also, I *am* longing to see the babies. How nice of Rix to be like me!"

"He must be a discerning youth," laughed the doctor, with an admiring glance at his charming wife. "Mollie will have her hands full with those three kiddies!"

"Oh, she'll have an ayah for them," said Madge easily. "Well, what are we going to do with ourselves now?"

"Let's play at something," suggested Joey. "The Robin will have to go to bed soon."

"There are yet two hours," protested the Robin.

"Well, two hours goes jolly fast when it's near bedtime," declared Joey. "What would you like to play at?"

"Walking Up the Hill-side," decided the Robin. "Oh! Here comes papa!" She ran to meet her father, who picked her up, and came into the room with her on his shoulder. He was smiling as he came, and Joey thought, not for the first time, that "Uncle Ted" was a dear when he looked like that.

"I've some news for you all," he said as he sat down, transferring his little daughter to his knee. "You may have three guesses among you."

"An expedition tomorrow," said Jo instantly.

"That's right as far as it goes. But you must get nearer than that, Joey."

"We are going to Salzburg," said Grizel instantly. It was a long-desired trip, and had been promised to them for some time.

"Clever girl! Yes; I saw the Lannisses today, and Mr Lannis has to go over on business. He offers to take you three and Mrs Russell if she can come."

"The children may go," replied Madge. "I'm afraid I can't."

"Oh, Madge! Why not?" Jo's voice was full of disappointment.

"I'm sorry, Jo, but I haven't the time. What arrangements did you make with Mr Lannis, Captain Humphries?"

"I said we would ring them up and let them know," replied the captain. "He is going by car, and is taking Evadne. If the children may go, he will meet us at the foot of the mountain at nine o'clock. They must bring things for the night, as he thinks it is too far to go and come in one day, and his business may take a little time. Mrs Lannis is not going, but her French maid will be there, so that the girls won't be left alone while he is at his meeting. He hoped you would go, Mrs Russell; but if you couldn't, he says Suzette is quite capable of looking after them. They will, of course, promise to do as she says.'' He glanced down at his own little girl, who nodded her curly head. ''Me, I will be very good, papa; I will do all Suzette tells me.''

''And the others?'' He looked across at Joey and Grizel.

''Oh, rather!'' said Jo. ''I'll be an angel without wings if you let us go, Madge.''

Madge laughed. ''If you are, it'll be the first time, and I can *not* imagine you being angelic on any occasion, Jo. Still, I feel sure you will do as you are told, and not give Mr Lannis any trouble.''

''I'll look after them,'' promised Grizel, and Madge was satisfied. She knew that if Grizel kept the other two out of mischief, she would necessarily keep out of mischief herself.

So it was arranged, and as soon as Captain Humphries had had his coffee, he went off to ring up the hotel where the Lannisses were staying and tell them that the girls would come.

As for those young ladies themselves, they rushed upstairs to pack a small case with their belongings as soon as the meal was over. Madge followed to suggest early bed, since they would have to be up by five the next morning, and would have a full day. She drew Grizel to one side while the other two were joyfully arguing about their trip.

''Grizel, I want you to promise me that you will try to see that the Robin is in bed by eight o'clock at latest. I know that Evadne sits up to all hours at home, and I expect you and Jo will not get off before ten. But the Robin *must* go as near her usual time as possible. It won't hurt Jo to sit up for once, and, of course, you are much older, and ten is not too late in holiday times when you are not working, and can sleep later the next morning. But the Robin would be worn out for the rest of the week if it was permitted her. Will you see to it, dear?''

Grizel nodded. "Yes, of course I will, Madame."

"I'm sorry to burden you with all this responsibility, Grizel; but after all, if I can't trust my head girl, whom can I trust?"

"I'll do my honest best," promised Grizel, a little more colour than usual touching her pretty face. "I can't do more."

"Then I can let you all go quite happily," said her Head with a smile. "You are a great comfort to me, Grizel. I feel I can trust you with them anywhere."

The commendation was deserved, for that term had shown that Grizel, when she put her mind to it, could be as trustworthy and as steady as ever Gisela or Juliet had been. Jo had taken good care that everyone should know how the head girl had tried to send her off with Robin, and face the maniac alone, and it had been Grizel's doing that they had got off as they had. Madge felt that the turning-point in the girl's career had come when they had resolved to give her one more chance, and was glad that she had done so; and though she had had a good many qualms at first, she was proud of Grizel now.

There was no chance of saying anything more, for Joey and the Robin came racing up at that minute to demand if it was really necessary to take an extra pair of stockings, as Marie Pfeiffen, who had come to help them, insisted.

"It'll be such a bore carting all that along!" said Jo.

"Well, if you don't take the stockings, it will mean that you'll have to stay at the hotel if you get your feet wet. Of course, if you like that idea, you can leave the extra pair behind. But you may please yourself about it." Eventually the stockings went in, though it entailed twenty minutes spent with a darning-needle, which had been her reason for objecting. Jo loathed mending, but she had no intention of spending the precious hours in Salzburg shut up in a hotel.

CHAPTER 14

Salzburg

Getting up early in the morning was not a favourite pastime of Grizel's, though Joey was usually an early riser. On this morning, however, the head girl was first out of bed, and was nearly dressed before Jo made any move. Madge was dressing the Robin, who was wild with excitement at the prospect of seeing Salzburg, and it was the faithful Marie who woke up Joey.

They were to go down as quickly as possible, for Mr Lannis had said he could not afford to wait, as his business appointment must be punctually kept, and he wanted to have lunch first. In the afternoon, while he was away, Suzette would take the girls to see the house where Mozart was born, now the Mozart Museum.

From there, they would go on to the cathedral, though Joey refused to be very much interested in it. Her favourite period of architecture was the Gothic, and the Salzburg Cathedral was built in the early part of the seventeenth century in the Italian baroque style, which she disliked. The Robin was anxious to see the famous fountain, the Hof-Brunnen in the Residencz-Platz, of which Amy Stevens had often told her. The Stevens had spent more than one winter in this beautiful town, and the great fountain had been Amy's favourite spot in it. Grizel had no special desires, and Evadne only wanted to go for the sake of the trip.

She greeted them joyfully when they arrived at the foot of the mountain, escorted by the doctor. "Say! Isn't this real nice?" she inquired, as she made room in the car.

"Gorgeous!" replied Jo ecstatically. "I'm dying to see Salzburg!"

"Your old Nap had a lot to do with it, I suppose? That's why you want to see it all so much, I guess. What I want is to hear that weird music thing at the Franciscan

Church, and they don't let females in — mean skunks!''

"*What* weird music thing?'' demanded Grizel.

"Don't remember its name, but I'm real mad to see it!''

"Well, if they don't let women in, I don't see you doing so,'' grinned Joey unsympathetically. After a pause she continued, "Oh, isn't this positively gorgeous? I love mountain scenery!''

Evadne looked out of the window casually. "It's not so dusty. I say, Joey, what d'you bet I get in and hear it, after all?''

"Nothing! You jolly well won't! Talk sense, Evadne, and let it alone! You'll only get run in if you try it on! They'd be safe to send for the *gendarmerie*. Don't make such an ass of yourself!''

Grizel, who had been staring out of the window, roused up to what was going on at this point, and demanded to know what they were talking about. Jo enlightened her, and she promptly squashed her hostess. "Don't be mad, Evadne! Do you want to let your father in for paying a big fine? For that's what it would come to.''

Evadne murmured something about "Poppa could afford it all right,'' but she ceased to discuss it, and the four returned to their gazing out of the window at the scenery.

It was very wonderful. At this point the road runs through mountains — the junction of the Tyrolean and Bavarian Alps, though they never crossed the frontier. Then it turns down into the Salzach valley, and follows the silver Salzach along till it reaches the suburbs of Salzburg. The suburbs are no more interesting than those of any other city, but in the great Mercedes-Benz they were soon left behind, and they came to old Salzburg, the great ecclesiastical city that generations of archbishops have built up on either side of the stream. On the east rises the great Kapuzinerberg hill, and on the west the city is flanked by the Mönschberg, both with wooded slopes, and houses nestling among the pines, larches, and silver birches.

The old houses, with their deep-red tiles and steeply sloping

119

roofs, make one think of fairy-tales; and the glimpses of the silver river, the old cobbled streets, and the views of the grim castle of Hohen-Salzburg, which can be caught now and then, all go to add to the impression.

Joey was wild with delight, and the Robin shared her joy, though the other two unromantically declared that they were hungry, and wanted lunch!

Their wishes were fulfilled almost immediately, for Mr Lannis drew up outside a restaurant on the far side of the river, and told them all to "come out, and get a hustle on about it."

Joey looked about her with a dissatisfied air, for they were now in modern surroundings, and there was nothing in her eyes that was interesting. The others pressed after the busy American into the restaurant, where they were served with a delicious meal.

"Well, Miss Joey, how do you like this place?" queried their host, as they ate soup full of macaroni and very delicious.

"It's awfully pretty, of course," said Joey, "but I love the old town that we came through to get here."

"Joey's mad on history, poppa," said Evadne. "I guess she doesn't think much to *this*!"

Mr Lannis laughed. "Why, we're right next door to the Schloss" — he pronounced it "slosh" — "Mirabell, which they reckon to be a fine sight, and chock-full of history."

"Oh, can we see it?" begged Jo eagerly.

"Why, I guess so. You'll like the gardens, anyway, and they have a wonderful aviary here. I can't take you myself, but Susie will look after you all, and tomorrow we'll go and visit the castle — if it's open on the Sabbath, which I guess it is in these parts. See here, Grizel, I'll give you the money now, and you all meet me at our hotel at six. You're to get your *Kaffee* at four as usual, and you can go shopping, for I want you should all take back a little gift to remember this visit. I guess there's enough there to give you each some spending-money, and the rest will pay for your sight-seeing

120

and *Kaffee und Kuchen*. Finished your soup? Hi, *Kellner*!''

The waiter came to change their plates, and serve them with tiny trout-like fish which were cooked in some wonderful sauce. It was followed by a fricassee of chicken and a pudding that made Evadne regret aloud that she had eaten so much of the other courses. They had coffee, and then Mr Lannis rose, paid the bill, and delivered them over to Suzette, whom he charged to take good care of them.

Suzette, taking the Robin's hand firmly, sent the other three on in front of her where she could keep an eye on them all the time, and they made their way to the entrance to the beautiful gardens of the Schloss, which the Archbishop Wolf Dietrich von Raitenau had had built for the lovely daughter of a Salzburg merchant in 1606. Grizel paid the small fee demanded, and they entered the grounds, where they were soon gasping with admiration. Here, in this sheltered part, the flowers bloom nearly all the year round, and at the end of March, when their own part of the country was just beginning to wake up, the beds were showing daffodils, narcissi, snowdrops, hyacinths, and many other spring flowers, while the velvety turf of the fine lawns was as green as if winter were not just ended. The place is almost a miracle of beauty, with long avenues, bordered by fine trees; ponds, fountains — at which the Robin cried delightedly — mazes, and beautiful groups of statuary. High above this, across the river, towers the huge fortress of the Hohen-Salzburg, like a grim sentinel keeping watch over a Sleeping Beauty.

''It's gorgeous!'' cried Jo. ''Fancy living here, and being able to come into this whenever you wanted to! What was the name of the lady? Anyone know?''

Nobody did, and she had to wait till they saw Mr Lannis again to learn that the lady's name had been Salome Alt, and that she had been a great friend of the archbishop's, who also had the credit of the great cathedral to his name.

At the aviary the Robin went nearly wild with delight, and insisted on staying there so long that it was nearly four before they could persuade her to leave it, and come to the town for *Kaffee und Kuchen*.

The town pleased them, though Joey declared that the shops were "rotten" compared with those of Vienna, which she knew well. Still, they got an excellent meal in a pretty Café Corso on the Gisela Kai, where they looked on to the silver river winding its way through the heart of the city, and feasted on wonderful cakes, with Suzette keeping a watchful eye on them all to see that they did not overdo it. She was very proud of her four charges, for Grizel, Evadne, and the Robin were pretty children, and Joey made up in distinction of appearance what she lacked in beauty.

When their appetites were satisfied they went shopping, and in the shops they found many charming things. Grizel bought Cooky a view of the cathedral, and also provided herself with some handkerchiefs embroidered with peasant embroidery for Mrs Russell. Evadne invested in a paper-knife adorned with a head of the great archbishop for her father, and presented Jo with a pen-holder wonderfully and weirdly carved. Jo bought postcards, a tiny ashtray for Jem, a doll for the Robin, and a collar for her sister; and the Robin, after many confabulations with all of them, spent her money on a pencil-case for the doctor, a brooch for his wife, handkerchiefs for the three girls, a collar for Suzette, a match-box for Mr Lannis, and a new tie for her father.

"Papa will like it, *n'est-ce pas*?" she said to Joey, displaying its glories of blue dashes on a mauve ground to them all.

"He'll be overcome," vowed Joey, when she had recovered her breath.

"You see," explained the small girl, "papa always wears such sad colours, so I thought he might like this. It is so pretty."

The thought of what Captain Humphries, who was always clad in dark things, and whose ties certainly bore no affinity to the lurid thing exposed to their view, would say on being informed that he was expected to wear it nearly convulsed

Grizel and Jo, though Evadne, not knowing him as they did, saw nothing to laugh at, and opened her eyes when Joey, with a feeble excuse about "something awfully funny in that policeman," gurgled wildly, and Grizel joined her.

"He's just like all of them, I guess," she said, after a prolonged scrutiny of the unconscious gendarme. "I don't see anything to laugh at about him."

"And it is not *comme il faut*," added Suzette severely. "Young ladies should not thus laugh in the street. They should be calm and well-behaved. Permit that I wrap up the cravat, *ma petite*, and let us now return to our hotel."

The Robin gave up the tie, and she folded it up inside its paper, and, with a final look of reproach, sent Evadne and Grizel on in front, keeping Jo and the Robin with her.

As the Robin was not permitted to sit up for dinner, they showed Mr Lannis their purchases before that, and he was highly gratified at their gifts. He was in a fine good humour, for his business had gone well. He told them that he was going to take them all to the theatre except the baby, and on the next day he would take them to the Mozart Museum and the cathedral, as well as the castle. Then the gong sounded for dinner, and the Robin trotted off to bed cheerfully, for Suzette had promised to sit beside her and tell her fairy-tales before she went to sleep, and Evadne had said that Suzette was a "ripper at stories! Guess she makes 'em up half the time, but they're *pie*!"

A pretty musical comedy from Vienna was under way when they reached the theatre, and the three girls enjoyed it immensely.

"One of the very nicest times I've ever known," said Jo, as she shook hands with Mr Lannis. "If tomorrow's like today's been, this will be a wonderful visit!"

However, much was to happen before then.

It was half-past two in the morning, and Jo was having wild dreams in which Archbishop Wolf Dietrich, Salome Alt, the play they had seen that night, and the Robin's gift to her father were all thoroughly mixed up, when a bell suddenly clanged out sharply, startling her awake at once. At the same time, there was a wild shriek of "Fire!" through the building, and a noise of people hastily and horrifyingly awakened from sleep. She started to her feet at once, grabbing the first garments that came handy, and struggling into them at top speed, while she shrieked to Grizel, who was sleeping in a bed in the opposite corner. Grizel tumbled out, and made for the electric switch, but in vain. She, too, grabbed her clothes, and got into them in hot haste, while Jo made for the door to get to the Robin. It was opened as she reached it, and Mr Lannis came in, the baby in his arms, Evadne following him, and Suzette, completely unnerved, and in wild hysterics, clinging to his arm. His face brightened as he saw, by the light of his electric torch, that the girls were awake and quite self-controlled. A wave of smoke came in with him, too, and they could hear the dull roaring of the fire, though, as yet, they could see no flames.

"Here, Grizel," he said sharply, "take the baby! There's a fire escape at the end of this corridor. Come along, all of you!"

He hustled them out, flinging an arm round Suzette, who screamed incessantly, and literally carrying her along the corridor, down which he ran, the children after him. They found the window to the escape blocked with people, many of them frantic with terror; and the noise of their cries, the agony in their faces, made the two English girls sick with horror. Evadne was crying quietly with fright, though she made no scene, only clung to Joey. The American realized that it would be dangerous to take the girls into that panic-stricken crowd, and turned back. He remembered having seen another escape at a window on the storey above them. Without a word he dragged Suzette along, the girls following him. Up the stairs they went, and came into a much narrower corridor. Here there was only one man, who was wrestling with the fastening of the window that gave on to the escape, and a fat, elderly woman. Awful as was their peril, Jo suddenly gave vent to a little giggle as she recognized her.

"It's Frau Berlin!" she said to Grizel. "We're always running into her at times like this."

Grizel, the Robin close in her arms, looked, and remembered the woman they had met during their first term at the chalet who had treated them so rudely, and whom Madge had later saved from a burning train when they were coming from the Dolomite district. Mr Lannis had dropped Suzette, who sank on the ground, moaning in terror, and made for the window, which he broke open with the first thing that came handy. Then he lifted Evadne out, and bade her go down as quickly as she could. Grizel put the Robin out next, and Jo followed. The American directed her to go on, and was turning back to pull Suzette up, when Frau Berlin made a dash, and clambered through the space, rushing down at a pace that was likely to endanger the lives of the children who were in front.

"Go on and stop her," said the strange man. "I will see to the woman."

Mr Lannis obeyed — there was no time for argument, for already the flames were beginning to lick through from the lower windows, and the girls were in fearful peril. He reached the frenzied woman just in time to stop her from trying to thrust Grizel aside, and, holding her in a grasp that bruised her, shouted to the girl to go on steadily, and keep to the outside handrail. Frau Berlin writhed and struggled in his grip, but he was a big man, luckily, and the thought of the harm she might do to the children gave him the strength to hold her, while his unknown friend got through with Suzette, and joined him.

None of them was likely to forget that journey down the iron stairs. By the time the two men with their charges had reached the first floor of the hotel the escape was almost wrapped in flames, and it was a miracle that they got through alive. Mr Lannis's first thought was for the girls. They were all standing at the bottom, in charge of one of the firemen, who was trying to get them away. The Robin had been thrust by Jo to the outside of the escape, and, with the elder child's skirt flung round her, was unhurt. Evadne and Jo were sights to behold, with their grimed faces and singed hair, but, save for one or two superficial burns, they were not damaged. Grizel was much worse off, though they did not know this till later on, when they were all retiring to bed in another hotel where they had taken refuge. She had been scorched by the flames, but not badly. The burns smarted, but she had reassured her host that she was all right; then when she put up her hands to tie back her hair, she gave a shriek, for a long curl came off in her fingers. Her cry was echoed by the other children, and Mr Lannis, very much bandaged, and still red-eyed from the smoke, came in to see what had happened. In the centre of the big room where the four were to sleep stood Grizel, holding her severed lock, while Jo and Evadne were standing aghast, and the Robin, from the bed where she had been tucked in by a now steadied and remorseful Suzette, was eyeing them with deep interest.

"What's got you all?" asked the big man.

For reply Grizel dropped her curl, put her hands to her head again, and literally ran off the lengthy locks. Then she stood there, denuded of her long hair, and looking scared. It had all been scorched in the flames as she had torn through them, and so had come off at the first tug.

Mr Lannis was horrified. At first he was afraid that her neck was burned, but the hair had saved it. Only − Grizel was fated not to put up her curls for some time to come. There was nothing to be done. Once he realized that the girls were really all right, Mr Lannis ordered them off to bed, and stayed there till they were safely between the sheets. In the morning he took Grizel to a hairdresser's and had her cropped, as that was the only thing to do. The hair had been scorched pretty close to her head, and was all uneven.

"What *will* Madge say when she sees you?" said Joey. "She'll have a fit, I should think!"

"She'll be so glad that we are all alive she will say

nothing," replied Grizel soberly. "If I hadn't shaken my hair over my face, *it* would have been burned, and I'd rather lose my hair than that."

"Oh, well, it'll be a saving of time in the morning," said her friend comfortingly. "But, *oh,* Grizel, you do look so different with it all gone!" She gave a hysterical little giggle.

Grizel shook her slightly. "Jo, shut up, you ass! Suzette's bad enough without *you* starting! You're to come and see if your new things will fit."

She and Mr Lannis had been shopping, for all their clothes had gone in the fire which had left their hotel completely gutted. He had insisted on refitting them, and, what was more, had bought their gifts over again, though the head girl had tried to stop him. Several coats and hats had been brought to their present resting-place for them to try on, and they were soon all fitted out, even down to underclothes, for they had all put on very little in their escape, and the Robin had had nothing but her pyjamas and dressing-gown.

When that business had been done, Mr Lannis marched them off to the station. He was not fit to drive the car, which had to be left in the garage till someone could bring it home. They were to be met at Spärtz by Dr Jem, to whom he had phoned, with the runabout, for the railway was not yet opened.

"What happened to Frau Berlin?" asked Joey as she sat down in her corner, the Robin cuddled close to her.

"Hanged if I know," replied Mr Lannis forcefully. "That woman should be shut up! She might have—" He paused and looked at them. He was doubtful how much they realized of the danger from the frantic woman.

Joey answered this unconsciously. "She might have fallen down and killed herself. I don't like her, but it would have been horrid if that had happened, and it might have done."

"She's a pie-faced, rubber-necked four-flusher," said Evadne. "Those railings were as open as anything. She'd have gone *some* crash if she *had* gone."

Grizel shivered slightly. She knew what danger had

threatened them all, if the others didn't. It wouldn't have been Frau Berlin who would have fallen through the railings. Mr Lannis noticed it and promptly began to talk about the history of Salzburg to divert her mind from the memory. He was so successful that twenty minutes later Jo and the head girl were well away with their old argument as to whether Napoleon was a great man or not, and they kept off dangerous topics for the rest of the journey, much to the American's relief.

CHAPTER 15

The New Term

"Matron, can I unpack now, please?"

"Please, Matron, which is to be the new girl's cubey in our dorm?"

"Matron, may I have the window cubey this term? *Do* say I may!"

"Please, Matron, Miss Maynard says if the new girl, Cornelia Flower, is unpacked, can she go to the study? If she isn't, can she go as soon as she *is*?"

Matron sat back on her heels and glared round the importunate throng. "If you don't all stop talking for five minutes," she remarked, "you'll drive me into the nearest lunatic asylum. Now, Jo, give me Miss Maynard's message again, please."

Like a parrot Jo repeated her message gravely, and the harassed lady who saw to the physical welfare of the Chalet School nodded. "Cornelia Flower is unpacked, and may go with you now. Her cubicle is Number Five; can you remember that, Cornelia?"

"Ya-as," drawled Cornelia, a fair, sturdy girl with enormous blue eyes.

"Then trot along with Jo. She can look after you for the present. — No, Evadne; you may *not* have a window cubicle. I know what that would mean! You will sleep in Number Seven, as you did last term. — Yes, Ilonka; I am ready to unpack you now, so come along, and don't waste time. — Paula and Frieda, you may be getting your cases opened; and, Simone, you can help to carry Ilonka's things to her cubicle."

Having thus disposed of her charges, Matron turned back to her work, and Jo walked off with Cornelia to the study, where Miss Maynard was waiting to interview her before deciding into which form to put her.

It was the last week of April, and the weather was gloriously fine, so when Joey had seen Cornelia close the study door after her, she wandered out into the flower garden, where she found her own special gang, with the exception of the people who were unpacking, all congregated together, and discussing the new term. Her appearance was hailed with cries of delight.

"Here comes Jo! Now she will tell us everything!" The speaker, Bianca di Ferrara, ran forward and linked her arm in her leader's. "Jo, we wish to know if it is true that Madame is not coming down to school at all this term? Luigia says that Grizel has said so."

"Yes; quite true," replied Jo. "Jem thinks the walk will be too much for her in the hot weather. So she's going to stay up at the Sonnalpe, where it will be cooler than down here."

"But, Jo, what happens about her birthday, then?" demanded Margia Stevens.

"Don't know, I'm sure! We'll have to have the 'do' without her, I suppose."

The girls looked at each other in dismay. Ever since Mrs Russell had come to the Tyrol and established her school on the shores of the Tiern See, they had kept her birthday as a festival, and the idea of not having her with them for it was one they did not relish.

"How very — not nice!" said Klara Melnarti at length, after a blank silence.

"Can't be helped! P'r'aps they'll have us there for it," suggested Jo. "Jem said he would think of it. It all depends."

"Oh, but that would be ravishing!" declared Bianca, beginning to smile. "Jo, Grizel said that we were to have some new girls this term. Do you know anything about them?"

"I've just carted Cornelia Flower off to Maynie," said Jo cheerfully.

"What is she like?" asked Klara. "She has a pretty name."

"Well, she doesn't live up to it — as far as looks go," said Jo. "She's nearly square, and she has a jaw like —

like — well, like a ramrod! About fourteen, I think, and she's in the Yellow dorm. Who's Head there this term? Anyone know?''

"Mary is, I think," said Bianca.

"Well, she's got a handful in Cornelia, or I'm blind! What possessed Matey to put two Americans in one dorm?

No one felt able to reply to this question, so they passed it over, and asked if Jo knew anything about the other new girls.

"Two more Middles — but they're to be day girls,'' was the response. "Sisters, who are at the Post with their people. And I believe the babes are getting one.''

"Then we are more than sixty this term,'' remarked Bianca with satisfaction. "That goes well! Of what nationality are the new girls, my Jo?''

"Bavarian,'' replied Jo. "They come from München, I think. Oh, and I've got some wonderful news for you all! Remember Marie Pfeiffen? Well, she's to be married next week, and we're all to go to the wedding! There's richness for you!''

A hurricane of exclamations of joy greeted this announcement. Many of the girls knew Marie very well, for she had been maid at the school for three years, only leaving it when her young mistress went to the Sonnalpe.

"Are we going to the dancing as well?'' demanded Margia, when they had calmed down a little.

"*Rather*! What do *you* think? That's the best part of it. We're to go for three hours, and I've promised to have a dance with Andreas!''

"Rot! How can you? You don't know the *Schuhplattler*!'' retorted Margia.

"I do! He and Marie taught us one during the hols. Grizel and I are going to teach you people, so that you can all do it. Besides, they are going to have some waltzes as well.''

"Mean to say we're going to lift great men off the ground like they do?'' asked Margia incredulously.

131

"Talk sense! This is one of the milder ones. Even the babes are to go for a while! There'll be some excitement, won't there?"

Bianca laughed. "There won't be any work done next week," she said. "When does the wedding take place?"

"On Thursday — a week today. Marie was awfully bucked with her present, by the way. She's hung it in her kitchen, and she's going to stick a table underneath, and keep flowers on it as long as she can. Isn't that nice of her?"

"Very nice indeed," said Bianca.

The Chalet School's gift had been a large group of the whole school, which they had had framed, and had sent up at the end of the previous term. Marie had been overjoyed at it — partly because one exactly the same hung in Madame's salon.

The group broke up after that, Jo going back to the study to see if Miss Maynard had finished with Cornelia, and the others scattering to various parts of the school grounds.

At the study door Jo encountered Grizel, who was coming in search of her, to tell her that Cornelia was waiting for her, and grinned at the head girl cheerfully. "Hello, Grizel! Haven't seen you since *Mittagessen*! What have you been doing?"

"A million things, I should think," said Grizel, running her fingers through her neatly-cropped hair — this departure had created quite a sensation already! — and heaving a sigh. "Miss Maynard has finished with Cornelia, Jo, and sent me to find you."

"Righto! I was just going to fetch her. Wonder where Maynie's put her."

"You'll know pretty soon, I expect. *Not* with Evadne, I hope, or prep *will* be a nightmare!" declared Grizel, who had suffered many things from Evadne during prep.

"Oh, Evvy's an ass," said Jo cheerfully. "Well, I'd better be pushing off, I s'pose."

"Yes; and while you're about it, I should advise a little less slang! Where you pick it all up, I can't think!"

"It must be in the atmosphere," returned Jo, as she tapped at the door.

Grizel went on, and left her to take charge of the new girl once more, which she did with the utmost cheerfulness.

"I have put Cornelia in the Lower Fourth for the present, Jo," said Miss Maynard. "Will you show her her form room, and introduce her to some of the other girls. You must make haste and learn some German and French, Cornelia, or you may not be able to talk at all meal-times."

"Ya-as," drawled Cornelia again. Then they went out, Jo dropping the little regulation curtsey, while the new girl stared at her, and walked soberly down the narrow passage to the big form room where two or three of the Lower Fourth were busily putting their desks in order for the morrow.

"D'you always do that?" asked Cornelia, as they went in.

"Do what?"

"Duck like that."

"Rather! It's manners all the time here, and so you'll jolly well find out."

Cornelia looked at her with limpid eyes that said nothing, and then followed her up to a little group where Evadne Lannis was holding forth about the hotel fire.

"Hi, Evvy! This is Cornelia Flower," said Jo, interrupting ruthlessly. "She's to be in your form, so you can look after her. These other people are Cyrilla Maurus, Giovanna Donati, Selma Khrakhovska, and Signa Johansen, Cornelia. They're all about your age, I think. Thirteen, aren't you?"

"Most fourteen," said Cornelia.

"Oh, then, that's all right. Which desk can she have, Giovanna?" She turned to Giovanna, the form-prefect the term before.

"That one by the window, Joey," said Giovanna in her soft, un-English voice. "We will all look after Cornelia."

"Thanks!" Joey turned on her heel, and left the room. She had a rooted objection to "doing sheepdog," and her theory was that new girls got on best if left to find their own feet. Perhaps if Cornelia had shown any signs of being nervous she would have stayed, but that was the last thing the new girl was. So Jo went off on some quest of her own.

Meanwhile, the Lower Fourth found to their joy that they had welcomed a genius into their midst. Cornelia was original when it came to sin, and she soon showed that she had no intention of being the form's conscience, or anything like that. On the contrary, she brightened them all up by her exploits, and they soon followed in her lead. Even Evadne, the self-sufficient, had to admit that the new girl could outdo them all in wickedness.

It was Cornelia who introduced into prep one of the harmless little green snakes they sometimes found outside, sending half the girls screaming on to the tops of their desks while Grizel, who was in charge, gingerly lifted the creature with a shovel borrowed from the kitchen for the purpose, and carried it off to the fence, over which she dropped it with a little suppressed scream.

She also suggested vaselining the blackboards, but Margia squelched that idea by the crushing remark, "We did that *ages* ago! You *are* behind the times!"

But it was she who mixed salt with the tooth-powder used by some of the Seniors, and it was this prank that brought about her own undoing. Grizel, on being informed by Dorota Heilinge and Eva von Heiling of what had occurred, held an inquiry, and found out the author of the misdeed, with the result that Cornelia went before a prefects' meeting, and startled them all into notice of herself by her calm impudence. As it was a first offence — so far as they knew — they let her off with a reprimand, and she went, not noticeably quenched at all.

"We must keep an eye on that kid," said Grizel when she had gone. "There's more in her than meets the eye!"

She fell foul of Jo Bettany on the third day of term, when she had a battle royal with Simone, and reduced that young lady to such a fury of weeping as drew even unsentimental Jo's attention. After sundry inquiries as to the cause of the squabble, Jo told Cornelia what she thought of her;

and as Jo's tongue could, on occasion, outdo anything even Grizel could produce, she got home more than once, and left the new girl mentally writhing. Not that Simone received much consolation from her friend. She was ordered "to stop being a sponge!" and taken off to play a slashing set of tennis which left her no time to brood over her wrongs. All the same, Jo was not going to have one of her special friends tormented by a "cheeky brat of a new girl". Cornelia, on her side, resolved to get even with Jo. But just then Marie's wedding intervened, and hostilities were postponed.

CHAPTER 16

Marie's Wedding

The Thursday morning of Marie Pfeiffen's wedding day dawned bright and clear. Usually, the Tyrolean peasant prefers to hold his wedding during the Carnival time in the winter. But Marie had been impressed by her young mistress's happy wedding day in the previous July, and had refused to be married at the usual time. Her bridegroom had backed her up in her request to hold their festival when the days were sunny, so they had braved local custom, and chosen May for their wedding day. In any case, Marie meant to have all the other details of her great day in accordance with the best traditions of the valley, and the girls knew, for they had been told, that there would be all the usual dancing, shooting matches, sports, and feasts that had from time immemorial been the leading features of a Tiernthal wedding.

Their invitations had duly come to them in envelopes tied with red and green ribbons, which they had all put away to keep as mementoes of the occasion. There would be no school, for the marriage service would take place at half-past nine. So at ten past they all walked down to the little white-washed chapel, clad in their white frocks, big white hats, and white shoes and stockings. They were solemnly escorted to seats near the front, and at half-past nine punctually the wedding party appeared.

Marie was attired in the dress of the valley — a short, full, red skirt, a black velvet bodice with full sleeves of white linen, and a lace kerchief knotted over the bodice. On her head was the wreath of rosemary which is worn in many of the Tyrol valleys by brides, and called by them "Mary's Flowers", in honour of the Virgin. Her bridegroom also wore his national costume, and they made a striking pair as they stood before the old white-haired priest who served all the churches round the Tiern See.

The service was not a long one, and presently they moved out to the fresh sunshine. At the door of the church stood two of the bride's brothers with huge bunches of artificial gold and silver flowers with which they presented those guests who were expected to come to the feast. The girls were all presented with one of the posies, and followed the bridal procession across the grass to the Kron Prinz Karl, where the feasting was to be. Herr Braun acted as host, for, in this valley, as in many others, the parents have as little to do with the actual arrangements as possible. A table had been set aside for the schoolgirls, and here they sat, and were feasted on strange foods. One dish consisted of pork, boiled in fat; another was of veal, cooked in some strange way, and adorned with slices of potatoes and cabbage; yet another was of bacon, cooked in butter, and served with spoonfuls of the butter poured over it. These were followed by dishes of dried figs, oranges, pears, and grapes, and the whole was — literally, as far as the villagers were concerned — washed down with huge mugs of beer. The girls were given tiny glasses of wine to drink, and then milky coffee.

The staff kept an anxious eye on their charges, for there was no saying how this unusual food would agree with them. Luckily, they were able to serve themselves by Herr Braun's special arrangement, so no one got more than a taste of any of the queer dishes. Joey, who hated fat, solaced herself on fruit, and several of the others did the same.

The villagers, meanwhile, ate steadily through enormous servings of the same things, and seemed no worse for it. Merry shoutings and laughter kept the whole room in an uproar, and it went on for two hours!

By this time most of the little ones were drowsy, but when a move was made to go into the other room where the musicians could already be heard playing softly, they roused up and followed with the rest.

The first business to attend to was the giving of the money gifts. Marie's godmother sat before a table on which stood a large dish, covered by a napkin. Her Uncle Gustav sat at one side, with a big sheet of paper, a pen, and a bottle of ink before him. The guests advanced, one by one, and slipped into the old dame's hand a small sum of money which she hid under the napkin, while the uncle wrote down the sum on the paper.

"What on earth is that for?" murmured Mary to Grizel.

"So that when there are any weddings in the guests' families, Marie and Andreas will know how much to give," replied Grizel cautiously. "Don't stare so, Mary! Your eyes look as if they were going to drop out!"

"Well, it's so weird!" retorted Mary. "Of all the businesslike ways of doing things! I don't think I quite like it."

"I think it's rather a good idea," said Deira, joining in the conversation. "You get what you give. Jolly neat, I think!"

Mary shook her head. She didn't approve, in spite of Grizel's murmured, "It's the custom, you ass! They've always done it!"

The girls had all been warned to bring money, so when the other guests had put in their contributions, they advanced and slipped their *Schillings* into the old lady's hand.

"She might look a bit more cheerful over it," murmured Jo to the faithful Simone, who was standing beside her. "It might be her own funeral she was attending!"

As the commentator was standing very near the lady, it was just as well that the latter had very little English, and didn't understand the remark, otherwise she would have been hurt. It is no part of the *Ehrenganger* to show gratification at the gifts. They are not for her, but for the wedded pair, and they must thank their friends — not she. When the giving was over, they passed on to where Marie and Andreas stood side by side, she with a glass of wine in her hand, he with a huge bun, both greasy and solid, with which the guests were presented as they left the "pay-table". The wine had to be drunk to the health of the newly wedded pair, and the bun was taken away to be eaten later.

Then the dancing began. And how those villagers did dance! Some of them were content with merely waltzing round and round; but some of the young men went in for far more spectacular doings. Jo was spinning round the room in the arms of good Herr Braun when one of Marie's younger uncles suddenly fell on his knees with a resounding bang, and, folding his arms across his breast, bent backwards till his head touched the ground, when he kept up a rhythmic tap-tapping with it, while his partner continued dancing round him. As suddenly as he had gone down, he sprang to his feet, his arms still folded, and, catching the pretty girl with whom he had been dancing, went on as if nothing had occurred.

Two or three athletic youths fell on their knees, and moved round and round on them, beating the floor in a way that made the girls ache for very sympathy, though these hardy young fellows made nothing of it, and after a minute or two of it would spring up, and go on waltzing as if they had never stopped.

"Goodness!" gasped Rosalie to Gertrud, with whom she was dancing. "Have they *any* skin left on their knees?"

The Tyrolean girl laughed. "Oh yes! They are accustomed to doing this, and they don't mind it. What you ought to see — only we cannot have it here, as the ceiling is so high — is the figure where the girl swings up her man and then goes on revolving, while he dances with his feet on the ceiling and his hands on her shoulders."

Rosalie stopped dead. "Are you pulling my leg?" she demanded.

Gertrud shook her pretty head. "No. It is really so. I have heard my father speak of it. I do not know if it is done in this valley; but I know it is in some. My father says that he has seen a couple dance like this for six minutes without stopping."

After about an hour of this kind of entertainment the musicians stopped playing, and one of the young men sprang up and sang a couple of lines, his partner standing beside him, her eyes modestly on the floor. Miss Maynard, who knew that sometimes these *Schnadahüpfler*, as they are called, are inclined to be questionable, was rather worried, but there was nothing to trouble her, and presently the orchestra went on. Jo, who had given the bridegroom his promised dance, and was rather weary now, slipped aside, and watched the trio with deep interest. There was a pipe, a zither, and a *Hackbrettel*. This last is a weird arrangement of bits of wood of various lengths and shapes, fixed on plaits of straw, and struck with a wooden mallet. Each gives out a different sound according to its size or form, and the result is not so bad as might be expected.

Finally, there was a little silence, in which people crowded back to the dining room to quench their thirst, and then began the *Ehrentanz*, which is danced by the bridal couple, the nearest of her relations, and any guests whom the bridegroom specially wishes to honour. The rest of the dancers crowd round the walls and watch it in silence, while the host and his wife stand near the musicians. As the couples waltz slowly round the room, these two present each with a full glass of wine, of which the lady sips a little. She then hands the rest over to her partner, who drains it. While this is going on, the brother of the bride sings a short rhyme in praise of his new brother-in-law as that worthy passes him every time he goes the round of the room. Sometimes this is turned into rather a rowdy affair, but on this occasion everyone liked the groom, so no one rose to challenge all that Fritzel Pfeiffen sang about Andreas.

Naturally Jo, Grizel, and the Robin were requested to join in the dancing, and so were Mademoiselle, Miss Maynard, and Miss Carthew. It is impossible to refuse without giving hurt to the feelings of the happy pair, so they joined in. When it was over, Marie and Andreas set out for their home, and the guests prepared to give themselves full swing. The girls also left the dancing room at the suggestion of Herr August, and went to watch the shooting matches, of which they soon tired. It was two o'clock by this time, and the sun was growing hot. Several of the little ones were tired out, and were inclined to be fractious, so Miss Carthew and Mademoiselle took them off home, where they were sent to bed, and left to have a quiet nap till four o'clock. The others stayed where they were or wandered about on the grass, where several couples, temporarily tired of the dancing, were doing likewise.

Among them was Herr August, as they all called him, to distinguish him from his brother, Herr Pfeiffen. He was one of the men on the little steamboats which run on the Tiern See in the summer, and the girls knew him well, and liked him immensely. Evadne, Jo, Margia, Simone, Paula, Frieda, and Cornelia, who had patched up a temporary peace with Jo, ran up to him when they saw him by himself, and demanded accounts of other weddings which he had attended. He was very willing to accede to their requests, and sat down with them round him, and told them stories of shooting matches and *Schuhplattler* exhibitions, in which the most marvellous feats had been performed.

When he had exhausted his repertoire, he sat silent for a minute. Then he turned to Jo. "Fräulein Joey, I have heard that the demon who tried to bear away the little Fräulein Robin has been seen again of late."

Jo sat up — she had been lounging against Frieda — and demanded, "Where?"

"Up on the haunted glen. He is as you say — tall, and with white hair and very blue eyes. He wears deerskins, and has neither hat nor shoes, and he dances and sings all the while."

"Horrid old thing!" said Jo, with an involuntary shudder.

"Who is it?" asked Cornelia, who had not heard of this before.

They nearly fell over themselves to tell her, till Joey, shrieking above the others, induced them to be quiet and let her tell it. She told it as well as she had told those legends during the previous term, and, hot day as it was, Margia averred that her blood ran cold at Jo's description of the maniac's anger when they had sent Rufus off with the Robin.

Cornelia listened with bated breath. "What an adventure," she said.

"It was indeed a terrible happening," said Herr August. "Luckily Our Blessed Lady was watching over *das Engelkind*, and so saved her from being dragged down to the demon's lair."

"It wasn't!" cried Frieda indignantly. "I mean, it was Grizel and Joey who saved her! Our Lady helped them, but they were there!"

"Ah, but it was our dear Lord and His Holy Mother who prompted the thought to take the dog," said Herr August, who possessed the simple, unquestioning faith of his race. "I think, too, that They watched over *die Fräulein* in their hour of peril, and saved them from the wrath of the demon."

"I'm jolly *sure* it was God," said Jo, in her own language. "If He hadn't been with us all the time, goodness only knows *what* would have happened!"

"Joey," said Margia abruptly, "what do you think that cleft was?"

"A hole in the mountains," responded Jo promptly.

"Yes; but *what* hole?"

"Why, just any hole! What d'you mean? Are you driving at something?"

"Well, I don't *know*, of course, but—" Margia paused.

"But — what? Oh, get on," cried Jo impatiently. "What's your idea — if you've *got* one, that is!"

Margia looked at them all. Herr August had got up, and sauntered off, seeing that the little ladies were well occupied. They were all literally hanging on her words.

"Get on!" said Jo again. "What is it?"

"Well," began Margia, "do you remember what Marie said Wanda's fiancé's father said about our lake?"

Jo shook her head. "No — oh yes, though, I do! He said that there were some wonderful caves either near it or under it. D'you mean, Margia, that you think that hole was the way in?"

"Well, it looks rather like it, doesn't it? It's in the part they all swear is haunted. None of the lake folk will go near it. You heard what Herr August thought of that old looney? I'll bet you what you like that's the way into the caves, and he lives there."

There was a thrilled silence after she had finished speaking. Then Jo spoke slowly. "I see what you mean. If one of them is all glittering and crystally, he might think it was Fairyland. That's why he's got that crack-brained notion about taking our Robin there. Oh, Margia! Supposing he had! Supposing we *hadn't* got there in time?"

"Well, you did," said Margia, in matter-of-fact tones, for Jo looked rather as if she might cry. "The thing is; if that's the way, then the caves can be found; and if they're safe, they can be used as you said."

"Oh!" Jo sat up again, her face blazing at the thought. "And it's *us* — it's the school that will have helped to discover them! Oh, Margia! You brain!"

"Come along, you people! I've been yelling at you till I'm hoarse! Why on earth can't you listen, you little nuisances?" It was Grizel, of course, and an irritated Grizel, who had to walk across from the other side of the pasture under the blazing sun.

They got meekly to their feet, but, just as Jo was about to announce their glorious idea, the head girl cut in with, "Now don't talk! Come along! It's nearly four o'clock, and we have to get *Kaffee und Kuchen* for ourselves today."

When they reached the chalet they found the rest bringing their afternoon meal into the flower garden, and setting the tables in the shade of the two big trees that grew at one end of it.

"Come, children!" cried Miss Maynard, as she saw them. "Run along and change your frocks, and then come and help. What *has* made you so long in coming?"

She did not pause for an answer, and they went off to change before they came downstairs to help bring out the china and cakes. Then the little ones came racing across from

Le Petit Chalet, and since mention of the Robin's adventure before any of them had been banned, they were obliged to be silent.

The chances are, however, that they would have discussed it some time during the evening, and the Seniors would have heard of it, in which case much might have been saved. But just as Mademoiselle was marshalling the little ones off to bed, Miss Maynard's brother appeared on the scene. He came straight across to Jo. "Go and get your hat," he said. "Put on strong shoes, and come at once."

Miss Maynard, who was standing near, turned white. "Jack! What is it?" she asked.

"Mrs Russell has a little son, born this morning, and she wants Jo," he said brusquely. Jo was off like a shot, and was back in almost less time than it takes to tell. They set out for the Sonnalpe, leaving a startled school behind them, and all thought of the caves passed completely out of the minds of everyone for the next twenty-four hours. It was not till a flushed and, wonderful to relate, tearful Jo reappeared on the scenes that they settled down to tranquility again.

She had very little to say, but she assured them that the baby was a darling, and Madge was all right — now. She was to go up again on Sunday, and stay for a few days, and they hoped that Grizel and the Robin would be able to go up two weeks later. That was all she would say, and she remained uncannily reserved and taciturn for her. When Cornelia referred to the caves, she shook her off. "Bother the old caves! I don't care a toss for them! Go away and leave me alone!"

Cornelia went; but the patched-up peace was at an end as far as she was concerned. She would take jolly good care to get her own back somehow!

CHAPTER 17

Rebellion

On the Sunday, Jo departed for the Sonnalpe, accompanied by Miss Maynard, who wanted to see her brother, and bearing a message from the school to her sister, as well as a big armful of flowers from the garden, which the girls had all joined in gathering. Grizel, the Robin and Miss Carthew escorted them to the landing where the Chalet School boat was moored, and saw them off, Miss Carthew calling after them that they were to stay as long as they wanted, since everything would go well in their absence, while Grizel waved her hand silently.

"Jo seems different since Thursday," she said to the mistress as they turned to go back.

Miss Carthew glanced at her. "Yes; she is beginning to grow up a little. But you needn't regret it, Grizel. We shall need some of our elder Middles to grow up, for so many of you big girls are leaving this term."

Grizel nodded. "I know," she said. "Gertrud, Luigia, Lisa, Eva, Dorota, and me. Rosalie may go too, if her people come home, as they were saying. That leaves very few of our original girls indeed. Jo will be sixteen next term, though it hasn't seemed possible till this last day or two. I think she will make a splendid Senior, don't you?"

"Yes," said Miss Carthew. "She has been very young for her age, of course, but this has made her older."

"Well, can you wonder? She adores Madame. We all do that, of course; but with Jo it's something much bigger."

"Someone else has grown tremendously this year, Grizel," said Miss Carthew, as she passed through the gate the head girl held open for her. "You have been a splendid head girl, dear. I don't know who will follow in your steps, but, whoever she is, she will have her work cut out to keep up with you four."

Grizel coloured. "Thank you, Miss Carthew," she said simply. "I *have* tried."

"And succeeded." The mistress laid her arm round the slender shoulders of the girl at her side. "I am only sorry I shall not be here next term to see how the school goes on when you, the last of the original 'big' girls, have left."

Grizel sighed. "That's the worst of getting fond of a place! You have to leave it. But after all, Miss Carthew, you are going because you are getting married. I've got to go because my people say so. Well, I've had four gorgeous years, and after all — I'm almost eighteen now; week after next I shall be — I suppose I've had my fair share of school life. But I wish it wasn't coming to an end. I'd give worlds if I could think I might come back here to teach! But I never shall. I wouldn't teach music for anything on this earth, and father won't let me have a physical training. He won't even let me go to the Royal Holloway College to read maths. I did think he would agree to that, but he won't. It's to be two years in Florence, and then home, I suppose!"

Miss Carthew looked down at the pretty face at her shoulder. She was a very tall woman, and Grizel was small. Her curly crop somehow made her look older than the floating curls had done, and the mistress realized that the girl was growing up, almost as fast as Joey. "Things may turn out differently, Grizel," she said gently. "In two years' time you will be twenty. Other things may have come into your life by that time — you might not want to come back."

"Do you mean I might want to marry?" asked Grizel. "I don't think so, Miss Carthew. I can't imagine it anyway."

"Not now; and it's as well not to worry about it till it comes — if it does. But if it does, Grizel, it's one of the ends for which God made woman. Never forget that. Madame loved her school. She still loves it, But I think she would tell you that she is happier now than she ever thought she could be."

She changed the subject after that, but Grizel referred to

146

it when they went in at the summons of the bell for *Frühstück*.
"I will remember, Miss Carthew," she said. "Thanks for what you said just now."

They went in to find Cornelia and Frieda in the middle of a battle royal — a rare thing for quiet Frieda, who lived up to the meaning of her name on most occasions, and had earned for herself the title of "Peacemaker".

Frieda wouldn't, and Cornelia scarcely dared say what was wrong, so Grizel had to content herself with administering a conduct mark apiece to them, and sending them into *Frühstück* with the remark that they ought to be ashamed.

"I'm not!" said Cornelia defiantly.

"Then you ought!" snapped Frieda, so surprisingly, that Grizel nearly sent her to Matron to have her temperature taken. It was so unlike Frieda.

Cornelia contented herself by pulling a face at her adversary, and Grizel thought it wiser to take no further notice.

"Cornelia's a perfect little brute," she thought, as she ate her rolls and honey. "Just like I used to be. Mercy, Simone! What *is* the matter?" For Simone had suddenly dissolved into tears.

Matron, who was sitting at the next table, took matters in hand at once. She had been glancing across, wondering what made the head girl so grave, and she had caught sight of Cornelia administering a sharp nip to her next-door neighbour.

"Mademoiselle, will you excuse Cornelia?" she said, rising.

"Certainly, Matron," said Mademoiselle, who at the distant staff table had seen nothing. "Go with Matron, Cornelia. Simone, why do you weep?"

Simone pulled herself together, and murmured something unintelligible to anyone. Seeing that she appeared to be all right, Mademoiselle ceased her inquiries. She knew her young cousin to be given to tears on all occasions, and came to the conclusion that the child was missing Joey. That

Matron's abstraction of Cornelia had anything to do with it never struck her at the time.

Meanwhile the new girl was marched off by Matron, and up to the sick room, where she was ordered to undress and go to bed.

"Why?" she demanded.

"You know well enough why," retorted Matron. "If you really don't, you can spend your time between now and *Mittagessen* in finding out! For sheer unpleasant, cowardly tricks, Cornelia Flower, you beat everything. A good whipping is what you deserve!"

Cornelia dared say no more. Matron was a martinet, and, well, that pinch bestowed on Simone would have an unpleasant sound if it were retailed to Mademoiselle. She undressed herself sulkily and got into bed, while Matron closed the shutters after opening the slats to let the air in.

"There you stay till one o'clock," she said grimly, when she had seen Cornelia between the sheets. "If ever I catch you at such a nasty thing again, miss, I'll take you straight to Mademoiselle! And don't you dare to stir till I give you permission!"

With that she marched out, closing the door behind her, and leaving a thoroughly rebellious Cornelia to toss about and listen to the gay voices of the others as they wandered about the grounds in the interval before they went to church. She would have set Matron at defiance if she had dared. But even Cornelia the rebel drew the line at that. They were all rather in awe of Matron, and she was no exception to the rule. So she stayed there all through the pleasant, sunny hours, thinking how she could revenge herself on Jo, Matron, Frieda, Simone, and Grizel, whom she quite unfairly included in her vendetta, since that young lady had had no idea as to why she had been suddenly deprived of the American girl, and was still wondering, since Matron had given her no explanation.

To Mademoiselle, Matron had simply said that Cornelia was behaving very badly at table, and she had sent her to bed as punishment. Mademoiselle, her thoughts elsewhere, had scarcely listened, and merely replied that it was all right.

The greater part of the school was, of course, Roman Catholic, so only a very few were present in the big school room for the service they had there, and inquiries as to Cornelia's whereabouts were only answered by Grizel's statement that Matron knew about it. When service was over the girls once more went into the garden. Most of them got chairs and books, and read quietly till the others came home. But Mary Burnett, Margia and Amy Stevens, and Signa Johansen elected to bring cushions, and sit under the great lime tree that grew near the sick room window. On the still air their voices floated up and, even as Grizel herself had done long since, she heard their opinion of her stated in clear unvarnished terms.

"I don't like Cornelia," said Amy, apparently *à propos* of nothing; for Margia answered, "Who on earth asked you to? And what makes you drag *her* up so suddenly?"

"Well, I was wondering where she was," explained Amy. "No one's seen her since Matey hauled her out from *Frühstück.*"

"She's no loss," declared Mary. "She's an absolute little brute. Evadne's a monkey, but she's straight enough!"

"Cornelia tells lies," observed Amy slowly.

"She cheats," added Margia, who had already had one battle with Cornelia over the question.

"It's a jolly good thing she's not a Guide! She'd let us down wholesale!"

"Perhaps it's Guides she needs," suggested Mary. "After all, Margia, that's what Guides are *for* — to help people to play straight."

Grizel's voice was to be heard at this juncture calling Mary, so she evidently went, for Cornelia heard no more. However, Signa had something to say on the subject. "Is it because Cornelia is American and not English that she does not play the game?"

"Rats!" said Margia. "That's got nothing to do with it!

Evvy's American, and she's as straight as a die! No; it's just general nastiness.''

They must have gone away after this, for Cornelia heard no more, but what she *had* heard had roused every bad feeling in her. She literally squirmed as she lay there, rubbing her fair hair out of her eyes. ''The caves!'' she said aloud. ''That's how I can get back at them!''

Till that moment she had never given another thought to the caves since Thursday, which had been so eventful. Now they came rushing back to her memory. She knew no more than she had heard on that day, but she had realized then that they were of enormous importance to Jo. She had said something about the school having discovered them. Well, if she, Cornelia, were to go and find out the way herself, it wouldn't be the school, because she meant to write to her father and ask him to take her away at the end of the term. If she coaxed hard enough, she felt sure he would! Then, if she had to go and look for them, it would give the people in charge a nice fright when she wasn't to be found. It was a *lovely* plan!

She was so pleased with herself that she actually lay still, and when Matron came upstairs an hour later to tell her to get up and dress, she found the girl sound asleep. It took some shaking to waken her, but Matron accomplished it at last, and bade her hurry up and come downstairs. ''And just try and keep your hands to yourself for the future!'' she concluded.

Cornelia got up meekly, and dressed herself and came downstairs, looking, so Margia said, as if butter wouldn't melt in her mouth. Inwardly she was hugging herself with glee over her plan. She was very subdued for the rest of the day, and Matron, watching her, congratulated herself on having found a method of subduing a most unsubduable child. But all the time she was watching her opportunity, and late in the afternoon, she managed to catch Marie von Eschenau alone, and asked her to come for a stroll.

Marie was a very nice child, but she was by no means

clever. She felt sorry for Cornelia, who had had such a bad morning of it, so she agreed, and by the time they came in, Cornelia knew as much as she did about those caves. She also knew just why Jo Bettany was so keen on finding them. Cornelia had never spent a winter here, so she was unable to appreciate the reason behind Jo's idea, and it struck the American child as "rather mad, but just like that horrid Jo!" She didn't say so to Marie, who would have been up in arms at once at the merest suggestion of it. All she *did* say was, "What a funny idea!"

"But I think it is a very good one," said Marie in her soft, pretty voice. "The people here are so poor, and such a sight would mean a great deal to them. So I hope Jo and Grizel find the caves, for that would be a very nice thing to be able to say that it was they who had done it; though I know they do not think of it that way."

Cornelia said nothing, and as the bell rang just then, summoning them to *Kaffee und Kuchen*, she had a good excuse for making no answer. But to herself she thought, "Oh, *will* they? I know better!"

CHAPTER 18

Joey Returns

Cornelia fully intended to carry out her great scheme as soon as possible, but various events occurred which it made it impossible. To begin with, she was watched carefully by Matron and the prefects. Matron's opinion of the young lady was that she was a little demon, and goodness knew what she would do if left to herself. The prefects' impression was that there was more in her than met the eye. Grizel, who had herself been a nuisance in the early days of the school, was aware that the American child was quite likely to break out sooner or later, so warned the others to be careful.

Time was fully planned out at the school, and, though the girls had a certain amount of freedom, there was also a good deal of supervision — more so than in many English boarding-schools. Besides, in the summer term there was always more to do, and the girls devoted a great deal of their time to games. These were compulsory, and had to be played in the evenings, as the afternoons in summer were very hot as a rule. Work began at half-past eight, and went on till a quarter to one. This included preparation periods. After *Mittagessen* there was an hour's rest, when they went to their cubicles and lay down. After that they had singing, sewing, handiwork, or music lessons. Then came *Kaffee und Kuchen*, and after that tennis or cricket. *Abendessen* was at seven, and when it was over, they were free till bed-time. Work was considerably lightened too, so that the short preparation periods might be sufficient, and all practice had to be done before *Frühstück*, which was at a quarter to eight.

Under these circumstances Cornelia found that it was not going to be easy to get away. This upset her so badly that she became a perfect nuisance in lessons — fidgeting, not attending, and answering the mistresses with so much impertinence when called to order that it was scarcely surprising that she found herself in the black books of the entire staff. Finally, she came into violent collision with Miss Maynard, and she was marched off to bed — the only punishment she appeared to mind — and there left to come to her senses.

It would have been a good opportunity for slipping off if Matron had not been working in the room across the passage, and there could be no question of her climbing down from the balcony, for the Lower Fourth's form room was immediately beneath the dormitory, and they would have seen her. Since getting away was out of the question, the young lady proceeded to revenge herself for her punishment by getting the sponges of the seven other people who slept in the same dormitory, soaking them thoroughly, and placing them in the exact centres of their owners' beds. Then she retired to her own, and lay looking again — for it was becoming a characteristic pose with her — as if butter wouldn't melt in her mouth.

Her suspicions aroused by the silence in the Yellow dormitory — the last time Cornelia had been sent to bed she had sung all the songs she knew at the top of her voice — Matron came in to see if all was right. So far as she could judge there was nothing wrong — except Cornelia's expression. *That* was too good to be true! Matron looked round the room sharply. Then her eye was caught by a spot of wet on Paula von Rothenfels's counterpane. She made a dive, threw back the clothes, and displayed a nicely soaked bed. Five minutes later all the beds had been taken to pieces, and there were the wet sponges. They had been there for half an hour, so the beds were thoroughly damp.

Just at that moment the bell rang for break, and Matron, popping her head out of the window, called to Margia Stevens to send Mademoiselle to her. "And at *once*!" she concluded. Then she turned back to where Cornelia was lying. "We'll see what Mademoiselle has to say to this, miss! Of all the outrageous things to do! You deserve a good sound whipping!"

And this is exactly what Mademoiselle thought when she surveyed the beds.

A long lecture, the confiscation of her pocket money for three weeks, gating to grounds, and five French fables to be learned and repeated to the irate Head of the school were among her punishment. But what she felt far more was Matron's decree that she should take all the beds and the bedding, put everything outside in the garden to dry, and, when it was ready, remake all the beds. The mattresses were to be hung over the balcony; the clothes to be carried downstairs, and spread out on the playing field. Finally, the mattresses were to be put into fresh covers, and Cornelia was to do it.

It took her all day, and Matron saw to it that she had nothing but dry bread and milk till it *was* done. What made this one of the sharpest parts of her punishment was the fact that Herr Marani came up from Innsbruck for a short visit, and brought with him a big basket of his wife's cakes for them.

Sitting on the floor of the dormitory, stitching at one of the hated covers, Cornelia shed bitter tears as she heard the others making merry over the cakes which they had with their *Kaffee* out-of-doors, as they usually did when the day was hot. She heard the Robin's exclamation of, ''Me, I love Herr Marani!'' followed by Maria's, ''Mamma has made these cakes even better than usual!'' and she looked with loathing at the plate of dry bread and the big cup of milk which Luise had brought up for her.

Her first idea was to go on a hunger strike, and refuse to eat what they had given her, but Matron's contemptuous ''Well, it won't hurt you to fast for once!'' put an end to *that*. With tears dripping saltily down her face, she swallowed the hated meal, and then turned again to her task. She would have rebelled against it if she had dared, but she knew that if she did Matron would keep her word, which was that she should have no play at all till it was done, and that she should also do the other beds which would be changed at the week-end. So she kept on, and by seven o'clock she put in the

154

last stitch, and that part of her punishment was over.

Miss Durrant came for her then, and made her wash her face and hands, brush her hair, and come for a walk along the lakeside. "You have had no exercise today," she said quietly, "and that will not do. Get your hat; the sun is still hot."

Cornelia did as she was told in sulky silence, but, as Miss Durrant had no idea of talking to her, her silence fell rather flat. She was out for an hour; then she was brought back, and sent to bed in the sick room, which was the only one of the rooms to be without a balcony, so there was no possible escape from it, for it opened into Matron's room, and that lady was popularly reported to sleep with one ear open.

Joey came back on the next day, and was promptly assailed by several people all wanting to know how Madame was; what the baby was like; and when they were going to see them both. She was willing to chatter now, but she still had that curiously older air. "Madge is splendid," she said, "and the baby's a dear! He's got the duckiest little hands and feet you ever saw, and heaps of soft, black hair."

"What are they going to call him?" asked Grizel.

"David, after my father," said Jo. "And James too, of course."

"David James Russell," said Simone, trying it over to see how it sounded. "I think it is very nice, Joey."

"Oh, so do I!" put in Evadne eagerly. "What will they call him for short?"

"David, of course. Madge objects to Dave, which was what Dr Maynard suggested. All the same," added the baby's aunt with a chuckle, "I bet he'll be Davy before very long!"

"But that is a pretty name too," said the Robin, who had been listening. "Joey, when are Grizel and I to see him? I do so want to see a very *little* baby!"

"The week after next," said Jo. "You and Grizel are to go up for the weekend, and I'm coming for the Sunday."

"But why not for the whole time with us?" objected Grizel.

"Madge says it wouldn't be fair. I've just had a week with

her, and she thinks I ought not to have any more than just a day till half term now."

"That's like Madame," said Mary. "She is the fairest person I've ever met, I think."

"We've some news for you — guess what?" chimed in Margia.

"Yes; make her guess!" laughed Rosalie. "Come along, Jo."

Jo thought hard, screwing up her mouth and frowning deeply the while. "Someone else is engaged," she hazarded.

"No! Not that! And who is there, anyway?"

"Well, Bette might!"

"At seventeen and a half? Talk sense, Joey!"

"There's Bernhilda."

"No; Bernhilda is not betrothed *yet*!" said Friedel, nodding her head as if she could tell secrets if she only would.

Jo was on her in a flash. "Do you mean she's going to? Who to?"

But Frieda only shook her head, and refused to state, in spite of all their eager entreaties.

"Well, they've put the trains on early, as it's such glorious weather."

"I don't think much of your guessing capacities!" said Grizel scornfully. "The trains *were* put on on Monday, but it won't make a lot of difference to us just now."

"Someone's coming to see us, then?"

"Ah, now you're getting at it. Yes; guess who."

"Elisaveta?" asked Jo excitedly, her mind going to this dear friend of hers.

"Elisaveta may be coming, but no one has told us of it," said Marie von Eschenau. "No; it's Wanda and Friedel."

"Marie! You little horror!" cried Rosalie. "You shouldn't have told!"

"Oh well, I was going to say them next," said Jo easily. "How wonderful! When are they coming, Marie?"

"On Friday. Tante Sofie is coming with them, and Wanda is to stay here, but Friedel is to go to the Kron Prinz Karl.

They are coming for three days while Tante Sofie visits her cousins in Innsbruck, and then they will go back with her.''

''Gorgeous! It will be nice to have Wanda again! Perhaps Gisela and Bernhilda could come too, and Bette as well! Then it would be almost like old times again! What do you think, Grizel?''

''Let's go and ask Mademoiselle. It's a splendid idea, Jo! If only Juliet could come, we should all be here at once, for Stephanie would come too. And as so many of us are leaving this term, I don't suppose we'll get another opportunity to be all together again.''

They trooped off to the flower garden, where the staff were taking their ease in deckchairs, and Jo proffered her request.

''I am glad you like the idea,'' said Mademoiselle, smiling. ''I have already written to our dear girls, and they are all coming, so Friday, Saturday, and Sunday we will make a little fête.''

Jo swung off her hat and waved it above her head. ''Three cheers for Mademoiselle!'' she cried. ''Come along, all of you!''

They cheered with a vim. Then, seeing that the staff probably wanted their free time to themselves, Grizel herded the noisy group away, and they went discussing the unexpected holiday in all its aspects. ''It won't be quite like old times, though,'' said Grizel with a sigh to Jo, when they were alone a little later on. ''Madame will not be with us.''

Jo followed the direction of her gaze towards the Sonnalpe, and nodded. ''No; but you can tell her all about it when you go up for the weekend.''

Grizel looked at her curiously. ''Jo! Don't you mind our going without you?''

Jo shook her head sturdily. ''Of course I don't. I've had a week with her — or five days, anyway. Of course, I haven't seen much of her; but I've been there, anyway. And I shall see lots of her later on!''

''And I shan't,'' sighed Grizel. ''I'm dreading Florence, Joey. I feel as if I should never come back, once I get there!''

"That's rot," said Jo. "You might as well say that when I go to Belsornia to be with Elisaveta *I* shall never come back! But I jolly well *shall*! I'll always come in the hols — and so must you!"

"It's different for you, Jo, You're sisters; I'm only a friend!"

Jo's black eyes grew soft. "You've been a good friend, Grizel. We'll want you, and you must come. Think of all we've done together."

Grizel turned away once more, and looked up at the beautiful mountain on the other side of the lake.

"We've been in some tight places, you and I," pursued Jo. "That makes us more than just ordinary friends, Griselda, my lamb."

"I'm glad you look on it like that, Jo. Oh, I'll come if I can! I don't often yarn, but you know how much I owe Madame and the Chalet School! It's been home to me these last four years."

"It can be home to you still," said Jo. "There's Evadne on the yell for us! What does she want *now*?"

Evadne came racing over the grass to them, shrieking their names as she came. "Gri-zel — Joey! Come on and play tennis! Rosalie's bagged the end court, and we're waiting!"

The two ran, glad on the whole for this interruption. Neither of them was in the habit of discussing her feelings, and both felt a little awkward about it, now that it was over. A fast set of tennis was just the thing they wanted.

It was also the thing they got. Rosalie was a steady player, and Evadne was brilliant on occasion, with a service which could be untakeable at times. Grizel was promising to be more than average, and Jo played a good average game, with odd flashes of inspiration and an uncanny gift for placing her balls, which made her a difficult opponent when she used it, as she did this evening.

The set finished, leaving Rosalie and Evadne as the victors with a score of nine-seven to their credit. Every point had been hotly contested, and the winners had only just got their two games.

"We're jolly good, aren't we?" said Jo most immodestly, as they walked together to the games shed to put away the balls. "That last service of yours was a brute, Evvy! I couldn't do a thing with it!"

"No one ever called you conceited, did they?" teased Rosalie.

Jo laughed. "I didn't mean it *quite* like that! But you must own that we aren't bad for schoolgirls, anyhow!"

"You'd be a good deal better if you'd only think what you were doing *all* the time instead of only occasionally," Grizel told her severely. "You can play decently when you try, but half the time you simply make wild swipes at the ball, and send it into the net or out of the court."

Jo did not look very much disturbed at this stricture, but she said, "Well, anyhow, *you* are awfully good, and Rosalie's as steady as old Time! We ought to have a very decent four this term!"

Then the bell rang for *Abendessen*, and they went in to struggle for a place at the Splasheries, and make themselves tidy.

CHAPTER 19

Cornelia Takes Her Chance

On the Friday Wanda von Eschenau and her betrothed arrived at three o'clock in the afternoon. Gisela, Bernhilda, and Bette had come up in the morning, and Stephanie from Lauterbach had walked to school in time for prayers. There were lessons for half the morning, then all work was at an end. A message had been sent down to Herr Anserl to say that the girls would not be having music lessons that afternoon, and Grizel, at any rate, had heaved a deep sigh of relief. "Thank goodness! I've scarcely looked at my Bach, and what I know about those Scriabin preludes would go into a nutshell! I must get up early and have a go at them tomorrow, for he'll expect them to be almost perfect by Tuesday."

Jo, whose music was of a very negligible quality, and who had patient Mademoiselle for a teacher, grinned. "If you mean those awful caterwauling things I heard you struggling with last night, I'm not surprised! There's neither tune nor meaning in them!"

"Oh yes, there is!" said Margia, who had learnt two of the preludes. "It's only because Grizel doesn't know them yet."

"The first one is a brute," declared Grizel. "Groups of three against groups of five! And he knows I hate contrary rhythms!"

"I wanted to do that one badly," said Margia wistfully, "but he wouldn't hear of it."

At this point in the conversation Evadne had dashed up to shriek excitedly that the boat was leaving Buchau at the other side, and there was a wild stampede to get hats and make for the Briesau landing, where they all stood waiting till the little lake steamer would come in.

After that there was little talk of work. The old girls were welcomed vociferously, and escorted back to the chalet, where they were regaled on cakes and lemonade, while everybody talked at once, and tried to tell them all that had happened during the term.

"And Madame, Joey?" said Gisela, when she could get in a word edgeways. "Maria told us when she wrote. How is she?"

"Very well," said Jo. "Just wait till you see David. Imagine it, Gisela, I have two nephews and two nieces! Isn't it priceless?"

Gisela looked at her with a smile. "It must be very pleasant. I am glad for you, Joey."

A wild shriek from Marie at this moment startled all of them.

"Marie! What has happened?" demanded Grizel. "Anything stung you?"

"No! But, oh Grizel! Just think! Kurt, my eldest brother, is betrothed!"

"What? Who to?" exclaimed Jo, with a great lack of grammar.

Grizel's eyes fell on Bernhilda's fair face, rosy with blushes. "Why, it's Bernhilda!" she cried.

"Bernie! *You*?" gasped Jo. "I say! How splendid!"

Poor shy Bernhilda scarcely knew which way to look as they all crowded round her, asking questions and discussing the latest excitement at the top of their voices.

"So *that's* what you were driving at the other night, Frieda," said Margia, when they had calmed down a little. "I say! aren't we growing up? Three of us engaged, and two going to be married soon! When are you going to do anything like that, Bette?"

Bette laughed, and shook her pretty head. "You must wait, Margia."

The arrival of the staff made fresh pandemonium, for everyone wanted to tell them the news. When they understood it, they wished Bernhilda every happiness, and she was the centre of attraction till Mademoiselle, having pity on her discomfort, suggested a move to the pine woods where they

161

were to picnic. "Some of you may go to meet Wanda and Herr von Glück by the three o'clock boat," she said. "And now, who will carry the baskets?"

They all made for the house to load themselves up, and presently they were struggling across the playing-field to the gate which led to the mountain slopes. The Middles had taken the food baskets; the Seniors carried the big cans of milk; and the Juniors bore long loaves of bread, which they would cut up when they began to eat. Everyone was responsible for her own mug, and the chalet was shut up for the day, Luise and Hansi going home for a short while.

"We've turned the people out of the Green dormy," said Grizel, who was walking with Bette, "and you people are to have your own old beds. Wanda is going into the Blue dormy where she was, Bianca being sent over to Le Petit Chalet. We shall be a full house this weekend! It's hard luck Juliet couldn't come, isn't it?"

"I am sorry she isn't here," agreed Gisela. "I am very fond of Juliet. And now, my Grizel, how does it go with you this term? Is all well?"

Grizel shood her head. "I can't exactly say that, Gisela. D'you see that fair, fat child walking with Evadne?"

Gisela looked in the direction she was indicating, and nodded. "Yes; what is wrong with her, Grizel?"

"She's the limit!" said Grizel. "Honestly, Gisela, she's hopeless. What do you think of this?" and she plunged into an account of Cornelia's last activities.

Gisela listened in startled silence. "But what a senseless thing to do!" she exclaimed.

"Yes! I was pretty bad in the old days, but I never did a mad thing like that," said Grizel. "And she's so untruthful too!"

"Ah, well, *that* you never were," said Gisela. "You were full of mischief, Grizel, but we all knew that we could rely on your word."

'Hi, there, you people! Don't you want any *Mittagessen*?" Mary Burnett hailed them at this moment, and they found that the others had settled on a little clearing and were already laying the cloth, and setting out the eatables. They made haste to join them, and presently they were all sitting round, and eating as if they hadn't seen food before that day.

"It's funny how much more one can eat out of doors than in," sighed Jo, as she began on her seventh sandwich.

"Yes; I notice you generally eat enough for three when we picnic," observed Margia.

"People who live in glass houses shouldn't throw stones. That's your fifth, anyhow! And Evadne is outdoing all of us!"

"Well, you aren't a bad second," laughed Miss Durrant, who was sitting near enough to hear them. "More milk, Robin?"

The Robin nodded her head — her mouth was too full for speech. The mistress attended to her wants, and then turned to see that Cornelia, who was sitting on the other side of her, had all she required.

Strictly speaking, Cornelia should not have been there, but it was not in Mademoiselle's heart to deprive her of the fête, and she had told her that the rest of her punishment should be remitted. "We do not wish that our old girls should have to see one of our present girls so punished, my child," the good lady had said gently. "So we will forgive you now, and you will try to do better, will you not?"

Cornelia had muttered something which might have been a promise to this effect. Mademoiselle hoped it was, and accepted it as such, so the young lady was out of durance vile and with the others once more. Her own friends still looked rather askance at her. They were a sinful crowd, but they had never aspired to the things she did, and, had they known what was at the back of her mind all the time, they would assuredly have cut her. After *Mittagessen* was over, and the baskets were re-packed, the girls sauntered off in twos and threes to gather flowers, hunt for early wild strawberries, and chatter about school affairs. The three old girls stayed with the staff, talking; and Grizel, Joey, Rosalie,

Mary, and Marie von Eschenau prepared to walk down to the boat-landing.

"Where's Paula?" demanded Joey just before they set off. "Oughtn't she to come too? Wanda's her cousin."

"She's over there with Cornelia and Evadne," said Mary, pointing. "Run and bring her, Joey."

Jo went off, and presently returned with the trio.

"Here, we don't want the entire crowd," protested Grizel. "You two run off and find the others. Paula may come if she likes; but not you, Evadne, nor you, Cornelia."

"Why not?" demanded Cornelia. "I want to see her."

"You'll see her when they get here. Now don't start making a fuss about it. Come along, you people. It's hot, and we don't want to hurry if we can help it. Go and join the others, Evadne and Cornelia."

It must be admitted that Grizel's tones were rather dictatorial, but she really felt out of patience with them. Cornelia, at any rate, had no right to ask to go. The head girl considered that she had done very well to be let off her punishment as it was.

Evadne turned away, with a growled "Guess I want to see Wanda as much as anyone!" Then she made off to join Frieda and Simone, who were looking for last year's pine-cones.

Cornelia sat down on a nearby stump, a gloomy frown on her face, and glared after the departing girls. She hated Grizel at that moment. She could have gone off if she liked then, for no one was watching her, but she had got it into her head that Herr von Glück might be able to tell her more about the caves than Marie knew.

"Silly kid!" commented Grizel, looking back and seeing her. "Come on, you folk! It's a good way to walk in this heat."

They strolled along, glad of the shade in the pines. When they reached the edge of the forest they would have to cross the open pastureland, and the sun was blazing down. The great limestone crags of the mountains glared white beneath its rays, and the Tiern See was blue as a piece of lapis lazuli. No breath of wind stirred its calm surface, and it was so still that their own voices sounded louder than usual.

"Ouf! It's hot!" panted Mary, who was scarlet with the heat. "If it's like this in May, what will it be like in June?"

"Well, June's nearly here," said Rosalie, who still contrived to keep cool and fresh. "Next Sunday will be the first. Oh, look! Isn't that the boat setting off from Seespitz? We'd better hurry a little."

"Heaps of time," said Grizel easily. "It's got to go to Buchau first, and it doesn't hurry itself."

Still, they broke into a trot, and managed to get to the landing just as the graceful little white steamer neared the moorings. Five minutes later they were welcoming Wanda and her fiancé. Herr Hauptmann Friedel von Glück was a tall, dark young man, with a pleasant face and a merry laugh, and it was obvious that he adored his lovely Wanda, who looked more like a fairy-tale princess than ever in her white frock and big shady hat. Jo made up her mind that he was nice; and while Wanda and Grizel went on ahead with Paula and the other two English girls, she and Marie escorted him over the meadowland and through the dark pines, chattering away all the time. The newly-arrived pair received quite a little ovation when they reached the picnic ground, and then everyone sat down to milk and cakes, while Wanda heard all the school news, and he was presented to various people of whom he had heard.

Cornelia, standing with Evadne, was introduced as "one of our American girls — this is the other." She was on her best behaviour for once, and her best behaviour was very charming. She soon induced the young man to talk of the caves, though he really knew little more than Marie, and the rest listened with deep interest.

"It would be so exciting if the entrance really could be discovered," said Mary, when he had finished.

"I think we've found it," said Jo quickly. Then she told them what she and Margia had discussed at Marie's wedding.

"It seems likely," he said, when she had finished. "As you say, the very fact that the villagers fear the spot would help to keep its secret through all these years. If it is so, then it is to you two that they will owe it. Herr Professor von der Witt is coming soon to see if he can find them. He is interested in the question, for he is a great geologist, as you may have heard."

"I do hope he finds the caves, and that they can be used for sight-seeing. But how will he manage? I'm certain none of the men round here will go near the place, even if they weren't all busy all the time," said Jo eagerly.

"He is bringing a party with him," said Herr von Glück. "I think he spoke of coming this weekend. We must bring him to see you — if Mademoiselle will permit," he bowed to Mademoiselle as he spoke; "then you and Fräulein Grizel can show him where your cleft is. That would save him a great deal of work, if it is really the entrance to the caves!"

"I'm sure it is," said Margia. "It's the only possible place."

"Could you show me whereabouts it is from here, Fräulein Grizel?" asked the captain.

Grizel got up from the log on which she had been sitting, and turned to the north. "It's over there, somewhere. Right below here, you know, and along nearly to where the river turns to enter the valley. I can't tell you exactly, but that's the direction. It is a long, narrow cleft. I don't think we'd have noticed it if we hadn't seen that awful old man and the Robin." She glanced round to make sure that none of the Juniors were anywhere near, but they had gone off on some business of their own, and there were only the Seniors and the Middles round them. "You cut across that grassland, and turn round to the left. It's right under the mountain, really. They say, you know, that that old lunatic has come back. Herr August told us at Marie's wedding."

"Only he called him a demon," added Jo. "They all think

he comes from hell, I believe, and I know they think he was going to carry off the Robin to hell!''

The return of the Juniors from their expedition put an end to the tale, and they all moved off in other directions. But *one* young person had heard all she wanted, and it would not be Cornelia's fault if she did not get ahead of them in finding the caves. ''And that'll be one in the eye for Joey and that pig Grizel!'' she thought complacently to herself. Her greatest difficulty would be in getting away. She must manage it through the night, if she could. Fortune favoured her for once. Matron, who had been looking rather white and poorly, now owned to a headache, which increased so that when they got home she was only fit for bed.

''You must go at once,'' said Miss Maynard. ''As for Cornelia — I'm sure you don't want a tiresome child next door to you tonight — she can go over to Le Petit Chalet for the night. I'll tell her to get her things.''

When Miss Maynard made up her mind to a thing it was generally done quickly. On this occasion Cornelia found herself bundled off to Le Petit Chalet, along with three or four other Middles, who had had to turn out to make room for the four old girls. Her joy when she found that she was given a window cubicle was great. She had managed to secrete her electric torch, and she went to bed with unusual serenity. One of her minor grievances against the school lay in the fact that she was not allowed to sit up as long as she chose, and she generally made a fuss about this. Tonight, however, she went off as quietly as the others, and unsuspicious Mademoiselle was under the impression that she was tired by the long day in the woods and took no notice of it, as Matron certainly would have done.

Cornelia waited till she heard the last door shut, keeping herself awake by sitting up in bed; and when she thought she had given everyone sufficient length of time to fall asleep, she got up, dressed herself with the utmost quietness, and climbed out of the window on to the balcony. From there it was an easy matter for her to drop to the ground, and then she set off at her best pace, making for the cleft in the rock of which the girls had spoken that afternoon; while Frieda, who had been disturbed by the sound of her drop, sat up and looked round her wonderingly. However, Frieda could not see through the curtains; she decided that it must have been a dream, and lay down again, and was soon fast asleep. Cornelia was not missed till *Frühstück* next morning, and by that time she was safely at the cleft, and making her way in, undeterred by any fears, though, had she known what was before her, she would have turned tail, and never stopped running until she was safely back at school.

CHAPTER 20

In The Caves

It was almost eight o'clock when Cornelia reached the cleft of which Jo and Grizel had spoken. She recognized it at once, long and narrow, and almost under the mountain. She was hungry, so she sat down and ate one of the apples she had bought at a chalet on her way. Then, throwing away the core, and cleansing her fingers by the simple method of licking them, she felt in her pocket to see that the two new batteries she had put there were all right, switched on her torch, and squeezed her way in.

She found herself in a dark, narrow passage, which went on as far as she could see. Walking warily, for she had no desire to tread on any snakes, and one *might* have made its home here, she went slowly along, her torch casting its bright light on the ground in front. For a long way the passage went fairly straight, then it suddenly took a sharp turn to the left, and she found that she was going downhill. It was quite dry underfoot, and as she went, the roof, which had been low at first, seemed to rise. There was no sound to be heard save the ring of her own feet on the hard ground, and many children would have been terrified. Not so Cornelia! She had made up her mind that she was going to discover those caves and discover them she would. Of what dangers might be ahead of her, she never even thought.

When she had been walking a long time — or so it seemed — she came to a kind of crossroads. This was the first check she had received, and she looked in dismay as she wondered which way she ought to take. She was tired now, for she had been up all night, and her legs were aching. With a little sigh, she sank down on the ground, and stared dismally round her. What should she do?

As if in answer to her question, one of the apples in her coat pocket rolled out, and trundled off on the path that led

169

to the left as it setting forth on a journey on its own account.

"I'll go that way," decided Cornelia, getting on to her weary feet again. "Of course, they said that the caves were probably under the lake, so this must be the path. But I wonder where the others go."

She stooped down, picked up the apple, which had come to rest against a hump in the ground, and walked on, munching as she went. She was dreadfully tired and only her indomitable will kept her going. Suddenly she tripped up over an unexpected depression in the earth, and fell headlong. She was not hurt, but she felt that she simply could not drag herself one step farther. She *must* rest a little before she went on!

She stretched herself out, sighing for very relief, and switched off her torch. The air was fairly fresh here, and she had sense enough to realize that she must not waste light. The thick darkness which descended on her dismayed her a little, but she argued that she didn't need a light to rest by. Then weariness did its work, and before she had grasped anything she was asleep.

For long hours she lay there, slumbering as peacefully as if she were in her own bed. She never heard light, stealthy steps coming along the passage, nor saw the flare of a rude torch of pinewood and resin. Neither did she feel herself lifted up in strong arms, and borne on steadily, while a cracked voice murmured exclamations of wonder over her. She had no knowledge of being carried for some two miles thus, and then being laid down on a heap of deerskins, while the strange being who had found her hung over her, and talked to himself in queer gutturals.

It was, in fact, nearly five o'clock when she awakened, and by that time the whole valley had been roused, and was out searching for her. Dr Jem had been summoned from the Sonnalpe, and had come down to hear that she had vanished. She had not gone *downwards*, for she had not been seen on any of the trains. Equally, no one had met her on the mountain path leading to Spärtz. The only clue they had to go on was that she had bought apples at one of the cottages on the way to Lauterbach; but that she had not gone on to the great Tiern Pass was proved, for a party of German students came that way, and they all agreed that they had seen nothing of a little girl with fair bobbed hair, a blue cotton frock, and a short brown coat.

"Can she have tried to go up the Tiernjoch?" questioned Grizel of Jo.

"Goodness knows," was Jo's gloomy response. "I don't *think* so though. She's not keen on climbing — you know the fuss she made about going up to the Bärenbad alpe."

Grizel flashed a quick glance at her. "Dr Jem won't tell Madame yet, Joey," she said.

"My goodness! I hope not!" returned Jo vigorously. "It would make her ill if she knew!"

Mademoiselle came up to them at this moment — a distraught Mademoiselle, with her hair untidy, and her face white. "Come, *mes enfants*. You must come and eat. Going without food will help no one!"

The two turned and followed her in from the garden where they had been talking. There was wisdom in her words, as they knew. They sat down at the table and ate their bread and butter, and drank their milk in silence, which even the talkative Middles didn't break. Once, towards the end of the meal, Marie turned to her next-door neighbour, Deira. "It's almost as if the Kobolds had carried her off," she said seriously.

"Ah, then, hold your tongue, will you?" said Deira in answer, and Marie obeyed.

When they had finished, the girls wandered out again, and roamed restlessly about the grounds. The younger Middles clustered together in the flower garden, and tried to think of *where* Cornelia could have gone. The rest just mooned about — to quote Mary Burnett — and did nothing.

The great fear in everyone's heart was that the child might have got herself into difficulties on one of the mountain slopes, and might be lying, even now, hurt and helpless. Their

171

main consolation was that she could not have fallen into the lake, since she had been going in the opposite direction. At nine o'clock the Middles were sent to bed, and the Seniors were made to follow at half-past. Only Grizel sat with the old girls, her face white with anxiety, while the staff still searched through the nearby pine woods, even Mademoiselle having gone with them.

Herr von Glück was with the five girls in the study, having just come back from a fruitless hunt through the woods across the little stream. He was tired and hungry, and Grizel had gone to the kitchen to get Luise to bring *Kaffee und Butterbrod* for him. She had just returned with her laden tray when there came the sound of bare feet running down the stairs, and then Joey, clad only in her pyjamas, and with her hair standing on end, burst into the room. She paid no need to anyone but Grizel, on whom she flung herself. "Grizel! I believe I know where she's gone! It's the caves! Don't you remember all the questions she's asked about them? Well, I believe she's gone off to try to find them on her own! Come on! I'm going to fetch her out!"

"Oh *no,* Joey!" It was Gisela who spoke, springing to her feet, and nearly overturning the tray the captain now held. "You must not! Think of what Madame would say!"

"I'm going," repeated Jo, her jaw set square. "I *am* thinking of Madame! If she knew about this, it would be enough to make her very ill. Grizel and I are the only two who know exactly where the entrance is, and, if we go, we can get there without wasting any time. She must be brought back before Madge has to hear about it, and I'm *going*!"

Herr von Glück set down the tray, and spoke with determination. "I will come with you, Fräulein Joey. What you say is right. Listen, Wanda." He turned to his betrothed. "I will take Fräulein Joey and Fräulein Grizel with me now, and we will set off at once. You must tell the others, and bid them to follow us. We will take string, so that we may leave a guiding cord for them to follow, and so that

172

we may not lose our way when we are returning. Fräulein Joey, go and dress at once, and put on thick shoes. You also, Fräulein Grizel. Fräulein Marani," he turned to Gisela, "you must find me some brandy. We may need it!"

The girls hurried off to do his bidding, and an hour later found the three who formed the vanguard of this wild expedition creeping along the mountain, hunting for the cleft.

Could poor terrified Cornelia have known how near they were, things would have been better. Unfortunately, she had no idea that help was coming, and it seemed to her as if she was alone − abandoned to the tender mercies of a maniac.

When she had awakened, shortly after five in the afternoon, it had been to find herself in a gigantic hollow place full of pillars that glittered in the light cast by rude torches which someone had lit and placed in holes here and there. The shape was nearly circular, and for a moment Cornelia lay and wondered if she were dreaming. She seemed to have got into some fairies' palace. Then, there was a movement near her, and, looking round, she repressed a scream with difficulty, for coming towards her was the man she recognized as being the lunatic of Grizel's and Joey's story of the Robin's rescue. He came softly, smiling at her, and with a strange light in his crazy blue eyes which scared her. "The gracious lady has slept long," he said in his soft, mumbling patois. "Almost I thought her under a spell, and would not open her eyes for a century. What does the gracious lady will that I, her servant, shall do for her?"

With a mighty effort Cornelia pulled herself together, and stood up. "Take me back," she said.

He shook his head with a cunning smile. "Nay, gracious lady. That may not be. They who come here are prisoners of the Kobolds and other fairy-folk. Anything but that!"

He had raised his voice as he spoke, and it boomed through the great pillared cave, echoing and re-echoing weirdly among the pillars. He came nearer as he spoke, and stretched out his hand to her. Cornelia shrank back against the pillar under which she had been lying. In her movement, she tripped over the deerskins which had formed her bed, and reeled, and would have fallen had not the maniac caught her, and set her gently on her feet again.

"The gracious lady must be careful," he said reproachfully. "You shiver, my little princess. Are you cold? Permit that I wrap this round you."

He picked up one of the skins, and drew it round her shoulders; then stooping, he picked her up, and carried her to the other side of the palace, where two pillars rose on each side of a mound, forming a kind of fantastic throne, on which he placed her.

How it was Cornelia managed to keep her senses was something no one was able to understand. Jo declared after it was all over that she would have died if it had been she. However, she *did* keep them, and, when he brought some bread and a handful of berries, she even managed to control herself sufficiently to take them and eat them. He brought her a wooden cup full of water, and she drank it thankfully. When her meal was over she felt better, and rose from her seat, anxious to explore.

She had been right in coming here, so far as the caves were concerned — she recognized that. Margia had been quite correct when she had guessed the cleft to be the entrance. Cornelia looked round her in wonder at the white, gleaming walls. What could it be? She thought it looked like diamonds. Wondering, she scraped her finger over the nearest pillar, and then took it to her lips. Salt! It was salt!

She knew of the great salt-mines in the Salzburg district at Hall, nearer to Innsbruck. It was evident that this was a kind of off-shoot from them, and, if this was so, then these caves would be of even more value to the people than Joey had imagined. She wondered where her strange host was, and glanced round. He had stolen on noiseless feet to a nearby pillar, and was standing there, watching her with a child-like smile of benevolence.

"I wish to go farther," she said in halting German, forcing her lips to utter the words.

He shook his head. "But no, gracious lady. That may not be. This is your home, little princess, and here you must dwell till the queen comes to you. But have no fear! I, Sigismund Arnolfi, will guard you, and keep all harm from you. Does the gracious lady will that I sing for her?"

Terrified lest she should rouse his anger, Cornelia agreed, and the strange creature took her hand in a claw-like grasp, and led her back to the throne, on which he seated her. Then from some niche he took down a zither, and, running his fingers across the strings, sounded a shower of silvery notes which the echoes took up, returning them in an elfin chorus of beauty which would have enchanted the child had she heard it under different circumstances. As it was, she had to clench her hands and set her teeth to keep herself from springing up and screaming.

The old man paid no heed to her. He lifted up his voice, and howled — no other word would describe the sounds he made! — a song about a beautiful lady and her true knight up to the vaulted roof. It was terrible; and the mocking echoes made it far worse. When he had finished it he started another, and he went on singing — or howling — for nearly two hours. After that he advanced once more to the thone, picked up the girl, and, carrying her over to the heap of deerskins on which she had wakened, laid her down.

"My little princess looks weary and must sleep," he said, covering her over very gently; but there was a strength in his hands which the terrified girl sensed rather than felt. She dared not dispute him. She lay submissively still, and when he had attended to the torches, and replaced with fresh ones those which were flickering to their death, he went and lay down himself before an opening which she rightly guessed to be the entrance to the passage. He was asleep in a minute, and his snores resounded through the cave.

Cornelia waited a full half-hour. Then got up cautiously, slipped off her shoes, and, carrying them in her hand, went towards another opening she had noticed when she had been wandering around the cave before. She had just reached it, when she suddenly heard a wild yell of rage, and, looking back, she saw him leaping across the floor to her. With a scream of uncontrollable terror she rushed through the entrance, and made off down a path which felt damp to her feet. She tore on, expecting every minute to feel his claw-like grasp on her shoulder. Suddenly, she crashed into something with stunning force. A blaze of stars followed; then thick darkness, and she knew no more.

CHAPTER 21

Rescue

How long she lay there unconscious, Cornelia never knew. She came to herself with a splitting headache, to find that she was very damp, and in a thick darkness that frightened her. She tried to get up, but her legs gave way under her, and her head throbbed so sickeningly that she was thankful to lie back again. She wondered, half-dazedly, how long she would have to lie there before help came. She never doubted but that help *would* come, sooner or later. She guessed that the school would be frantic about her being lost, and she had a hazy recollecion of the fact that Rufus had helped track the Robin. He would help find her, and then she would be taken back to the Chalet School. Once there, she would honestly behave herself, and be as good as she knew how.

"I'd just despise to be anything else!" she thought. "Oh, I wish my head would stop aching for a bit! How cold and damp it is! There must be a fog!"

By this time she was half-delirious, and had no idea that she was talking aloud. It had never crossed her mind to wonder why "Herr Arnolfi" hadn't come on her. She had forgotten all about him. By and by she fell into an uneasy slumber, in which she tossed and moaned, taking at intervals in rapid undertones.

It was a mercy for her that help was very near. At the moment when she had been making an effort to escape, Grizel, Joey, and Friedel von Glück were entering the cleft in the mountain side, and the young man was fastening one end of the first of the enormous balls of string which they had brought to a bush just outside. All three had torches, and all three had spare batteries with them. Friedel carried a tiny flask of brandy in one pocket and some bandages in the other, though the girls knew nothing of these. Time enough to tell them when they were needed, he thought. Joey had stuffed her pockets full of ripe gooseberries, which she had snatched from a dish in the Speisesaal, and Grizel had grabbed up some of the *Butterbrod* which Friedel had left from his hasty meal.

It was an easy journey till they came to the crossroads, but there they paused. Which way would the girl have taken? The two Guides hunted round for some sign, and Grizel uttered a sigh of relief when she found a small piece of apple-peeling, which Cornelia had dopped as she walked. "Here it is! This is the way she has gone!" she cried.

Friedel von Glück was at her side at once. "You will pardon that I lead the way, *mein Fräulein?* It is *necessary*!"

Grizel stared at him, but she squeezed herself against the wall and let him pass her. Then it struck her that he feared lest the lunatic might be in there with Cornelia, and, recognizing her as the saviour of the Robin, harm her. Meekly she followed him, insisting on Jo keeping behind her.

"It's — horribly dark!" said the latter impressionable young lady, with a shudder. "Don't get too far ahead, Grizel."

"All right, Joey," replied Grizel gently. "Grab my coat, and we'll keep together."

At this point the young captain stopped and demanded another ball of string. Grizel produced it, and rapidly knotted the two ends together with a reef-knot. Then they went on.

"We're going downhill," said Joey in low tones presently.

"I know," murmured the head girl in reply. "I'm certain now that Margia was right, and this *is* the way to the caves. I only hope we've enough string to last us!"

"Pardon that I ask that you do not talk," said their leader, stopping and turning round. "We cannot know how sound will carry in this place."

There was common sense in what he said, and they were silent as they went on. Presently they came to the place where

178

Cornelia had lain down to rest, and here they had proof of the fact that she was here, for on the ground was her torch, just as it had fallen from her relaxed grip when she had gone to sleep. Friedel von Glück picked it up and examined it. Her name was on a narrow band of silver round it, so there was no more doubt.

"Thank goodness!" thought Grizel. "But what a little ass!"

The path had been going downhill for some time, but now they found that it took a sharp turn upwards, and went out at a fairly steep gradient. Both girls were tired and the young captain was weary, too, for he had been out nearly all day hunting for the missing child. Their progress was slow, and Grizel, glancing round, was horrified at Jo's white face. They did not dare to pause, however. None of them could help thinking of the maniac who had tried to kidnap the Robin those few short months ago.

Suddenly Herr von Glück gave vent to a low exclamation and stopped. The girls stopped too, and crowded up to him. "There is a light ahead," he said, pointing.

They looked. Yes; it was true. A faint glow straight ahead of them told them that the first part of their journey was at an end. Rapidly the captain gave them their orders. They were to follow him till he said "Stop!" Then they were to stay where they were till they heard him call "Come!" If he called "Run!" they were to turn and run as quickly as they could till they came to the crossroads. There they were to turn to the right, extinguishing their torches, and go a little way down. If he did not come soon after that, they were to listen for sounds, and if all was quiet, to go back and follow the string till they got outside, where they were to go straight back to meet the search-party he felt sure would be hastening after them even now, and warn them that there was danger from the madman. He made them repeat his orders, and then led them on for another ten minutes. Then, short and sharp, came the order to stop. They stopped instantly, and he went on, while they crouched down by the wall, fearful of some unseen danger.

Jo was praying to herself very softly, but Grizel heard her. "Our Father Who art in Heaven, oh save us all from danger, and bring us back safe to the chalet!'

The elder girl bent her head. "Joey, let's say the 'Lighten our darkness,' " she whispered.

Jo began at once, and the murmured sound of the words strengthened them. When they had finished Grizel put her arm round Jo, and held her close. "I've *tried*!" she said. "You'll tell Madame, Joey."

"Yes," said Jo, "but I don't think there'll be any need, Grizel."

A long silence followed. Then Jo suddenly turned towards the elder girl. "Death — is just falling asleep to wake with God," she said softly.

"I know, Joey. It's just the memory of Madame's words that is helping me now."

Then they turned and faced what might be coming, calm with that thought.

Suddenly a call of "Come!" sounded through the passage. They started to their feet and bolted along to the glow. Suddenly they came on the great salt cave which had so filled Cornelia with wonder some hours since. The torches "Herr Arnolfi" had lit were beginning to die, but there was still enough light for them to see the glistening crystals, and Jo uttered an exclamation of admiration. In the centre of the cave, before a huge pillar, Herr von Glück was kneeling beside a dark heap. He seemed to be laying something white over part of it. Even as they looked he crossed himself and bent his head. A horrible fear that it was Cornelia, and that she was dead, came to Jo, and she swayed against Grizel, who caught her. "No, Joey! It's too big!" cried the elder girl. "It must be the lunatic."

Friedel von Glück, his brief prayer for the repose of the poor lost soul ended, rose to his feet. "It is safe now," he said gravely. "He died in my arms just before I called you. He says that the girl ran down the path that leads to the other caves — she is somewhere down there, and I am going to find her. Will you be afraid to stay here while I seek for her? I will not be long. He said he thought he heard her stumble, but he fell himself, and broke his leg in falling, or he would have gone to her. He struck his own head, and the double shock is what has killed him. He was very old, and I gather that his heart was not right. His senses had come back at the last, and he was able to tell me so much. Will you stay here, while I bring the other little one? You might say a prayer for the repose of his soul.''

Grizel nodded. ''Yes; we will stay. Go quickly and get Cornelia, please. Come, Joey; we will go over there to those skins, and wait.'' She lead Joey to the heap of deerskins on which Cornelia had lain, and made her lie down. Herr von Glück saw that they were all right, and went off on his final quest. Grizel held Joey close.

''Poor old thing!'' said the younger girl ''I am glad he is dead, Grizel!''

''So am I,'' said Grizel. Then she added softly, ''He has fallen asleep to wake with God.''

They lay there quietly, and presently both fell asleep. Friedel found them like that when he came back to the salt cave, carrying Cornelia who was now in a heavy stupor. He did not wake them, but he laid the other girl down beside them, and proceeded to bind up the nasty cut on her forehead, after scraping some salt from one of the pillars and rubbing it in. It was spartan treatment, but the best antiseptic he had at hand. The smarting of the salt on the open wound brought Cornelia to her senses, and she sat up with a low cry which awakened the other two. ''Oh, where are we?'' she wailed. ''What has happened? And oh, my head does hurt so!''

''It's all right, Cornelia,'' said Jo soothingly. ''You're quite safe and we're here with you. You must have banged your head a bit.''

''But the madman!'' cried Cornelia. ''Oh, he'll come and kill us all!''

Friedel pointed to the still figure with his handkerchief over its face. "He will never hurt anyone again," he said gently. "He is dead." Then he stripped off his coat and gave it to Grizel. "Her clothes are damp — that is a wet place. Undress her, and put that on her. Then I will wrap her up in one of the skins, and we must get her home as quickly as possible."

He moved over to the other side of the cave, out of sight, and they undressed her, and wrapped her in the coat. Grizel took off her own frock, and put that on her, too. Then they called to him, and he came and rolled her in one of the deer-skins. Just as he was about to lift her, they heard the tread of many feet and the sound of many voices. Lights showed at the entrance from the passage, and a throng of people poured into the cave. Mademoiselle was there, and Miss Maynard and Miss Durrant. Good Herr Braun from the Kron Prinz Karl, Dr Jem, Herr August, and — Joey rubbed her eyes in amazement, but it really was — Herr Anserl, looking more like a shaggy bear than ever with his long hair all tangled and untidy. There was also a big man who seemed to be vaguely familiar, and two or three others, who were armed with ropes and pickaxes. But she heeded none of them. Like a flash she had run across the floor, and was in her brother-in-law's arms. "Jem! Is Madge all right? She doesn't know?"

He caught her to him. "Jo! Thank God — thank God! No; she doesn't know!"

"We're all here," went on Joey, "only Cornelia has hurt her head. Herr Friedel has tied it up."

Jem set her down and hurried across to the little group. Then Joey found herself seized by a weeping Mademoiselle, who kissed her over and over again — rather to the young lady's disgust — and called her "*Chéri — ma mie — ma bien-amiée!*" till unsentimental Jo simply didn't know where to look. It was Grizel's turn after that, and while Miss Maynard helped the doctor to bandage Cornelia rather more scientifically than Herr von Glück had done it, the two girls were passed around among the company, and made to tell their story. Then the big man grabbed Joey — "Just as if I was a pick-pocket!" grumbled Jo later on — and demanded whether they knew where was the road to the other caves.

"Friedel knows," returned the young lady, dropping all formalities. "You'd better ask *him*!"

"What! Young Friedel *here*?" roared the big man. He let Jo go, and the next minute she saw him pouncing on Wanda's betrothed, and pouring out a perfect flood of questions. By this time Dr Jem had finished his work, and Miss Maynard was rolling Cornelia in a big shawl she had brought with her.

"Come," said the doctor, lifting up the bundle. "We must get back now."

"But I will stay!" roared the big man. "I am assured that we have the way, and I doubt not but that we shall make some marvellous discoveries! Here!" he turned to the men with the ropes and pickaxes, who had been standing to one side looking on. "Come, you! We go forward now! Do not wait for me, Herr Doktor! Take that imp of a child home, and those others, too. You may look for me some time on the morrow!"

With that he plunged down the path where Friedel had found Cornelia, the men following him, and was soon lost to sight, Jem laughed as he turned to the other entrance. "I suppose we must leave him to his discoveries. These children should be got to bed as soon as possible, and if I know Herr Professor von der Witt, no power on earth would turn him back now when he knows that the caves *must* be near!"

So *that* was who it was!

Then Herr Braun approached them, and with a "Pardon, *gnädiges Fräulein*!" picked up Joey in his arms, and strode off in the wake of the doctor, leaving Herr August to treat Grizel in precisely similar manner. The rest trooped after them, and they were carried in safety up the passage, and across the bush-grown turf till they came to the road where the path leads to the Tiern Pass, where they found three motors awaiting them. They were all bundled in, and then they set off. It was daylight by this time, and the sun was shining when Joey and Grizel, after a good meal, were finally tucked up in bed in their cubicles, and left to sleep off the effects of their latest escapade.

CHAPTER 22

"Three Cheers For Grizel!"

'I hate end of term when it's the summer term!'' Thus Joey, viciously.

Grizel Cochrame to whom she was speaking, looked at her seriously. "It's worse when it's your last term, Jo! And don't say anything to make it worse, my lamb! I will *not* make a sentimental ass of myself, but I can't answer for the consequences if you rub things in."

Jo cleared her throat. "Righto! — Oh, there's Rosa with David! Come on and see him!''

She turned and raced across the grass to where Rosa Pfeiffen was wheeling Master David Russell along in his white pram. Joey came up panting, for the day was hot, and hung over the pram, and made cooing noises to her small nephew, who lay looking at her with bland indifference, though when she slipped a finger into his dimpled paw he gripped tightly. "Isn't he a darling?'' said his adoring aunt.

"Jolly little chap,'' replied Grizel, peeping at him over her shoulder. "He's going to be awfully like Madame, Joey.''

"Yes; isn't he? I think he's rather like young Rix, too,'' replied Jo. Her brother had brought his family to the Tiern See three weeks ago, and the entire school had gone in for a course of baby-worship. Mrs Russell had come down with her small son to join them in the chalet Dick had taken for three months, and the girls had revelled in having their dear beloved Madame so near. Peggy and Rix were delightful small people, full of original sin; Baby Bridget proved to be "the *image* of Dick!'' to quote Joey; and little David was declared to beat them all by every girl in the school.

After that eventful night when they had rescued Cornelia the term had gone on fairly evenly. Cornelia had had a sharp attack of rheumatic fever as the result of lying in a damp place for many hours, but she was a tough little mortal, and had come through all right. The next event of importance had been Gisela's wedding, which had taken place in Innsbruck. The entire school had gone down for it, and had a remarkably good time. Then, on his mother's birthday David's christening feast had been the treat for this holiday. Finally, Wanda and Herr Hauptmann Friedel von Glück had been wedded a week ago, and were now enjoying their honeymoon at Partenkirchen in the Mittelwald.

The big event of the term, however, was the opening up of the caves, which proved to be wonderful beyond expectation. Herr von der Witt had found that the passage led right down to the first, which had the most marvellous stalactite formations, and thence to three others. In the last one were discovered relics of what must have formerly been a great city. Pavements and fragments of walls, all encrusted with lime, were there; excavations were going on, and more and more was being found each day. Jo was wildly excited about it all, for it proved that the legend of the lake's origin was no legend, but statement of fact. Experts who had come to see the place agreed that the lake must have risen quite suddenly and overwhelmed the city, though not, perhaps, quite as awfully as the old story said.

"It's been a full term," said Jo, when they at last turned away from the pram and strolled on up to the chalet. "What with one thing and another, I think it's been the fullest we've ever had."

"We've managed to crowd a good deal in," agreed Grizel. "I say! There's the bell for *Mittagessen!* Come on!"

They hurried in to take their places at the table, for there was to be a garden party that afternoon, and no one had much time to spare. Grizel took her place as head of the Junior table for the last time, and Jo went off to her own seat, where her beloved friend the little Crown Princess of Belsornia was waiting for her. Princess Elisaveta had gone to Vienna for Wanda's wedding, and then had come back to the school for the last week of the term, to wait for her dear Jo, who was to spend the summer holidays with her. She had come in to lessons, and had lived with the girls, just as she had done two terms ago when she had been one of themselves, and had delighted them all by vowing that it was a relief to be at school again. "Hurry up, Joey!" she said now. "We've got to dress yet, you know."

"I should think so," retorted Jo, with a glance at the crumpled frock the princess was wearing. "You look as if you had been put to bed in that cotton thing you've got on!"

"Well, you look as if you've been washing the floors in yours!" returned the princess.

"More potatoes, please, Simone."

Mrs Russell, in her old place at the head of the staff table glanced down the room with a smile. "How excited they all are! Just listen to Evadne screeching!"

"A good many of the others are doing their best to rival her," laughed Miss Maynard. "It must sound like a parrot house to anyone passing!"

"Oh well, it's the end of term," said Miss Carthew tolerantly. "You've got to allow for that."

"Oh, *I* don't mind," Miss Maynard assured her. 'I'm so thrilled about going home that I don't really mind what they do today."

"I also," put in Mademoiselle. "I know that our girls will never forget that they are of the Chalet School, and must not disgrace it, so I do not trouble if they are excited."

"Yes; even Cornelia seems to have learned that lesson," agreed Miss Maynard, with a glance to where that young person was sitting, much thinner than she had been, and still rather pale, but evidently very happy, and thoroughly one of them.

"I think we've all finished," said Miss Wilson at that moment.

Madge Russell nodded, and said grace. Then the girls were dismissed to their rooms to change into their prettiest frocks and make themselves as dainty as possible. There was a great deal of chatter as they changed, for many of them would

187

be going home with parents at the end of the afternoon, and all had much to say about holidays.

"Be sure you let us have your Florence address, Grizel," said Gertrud in the prefect's domitory. "You must write to us every week, and let us know what you are doing."

"And you must all write to *me*," said the head girl as she rapidly put a gloss on her short curls. "I shall be coming to Innsbruck for Bernhilda's wedding in December, you know, so I shall hope to see most of you then."

"And we will all come here for Madame's birthday next year," added Rosalie, who was going home to England, where her father had obtained a living in Kent. "We couldn't miss *that*!"

"Rather not!"

"Even Miss Carthew is coming for that, if she possibly can," put in Mary, who was looking forward to being head girl next term, and was wondering if she would ever be so good as any one of the four who had proceeded her.

Grizel threw down her brush and proceeded to wriggle into her frock. "Hurry up, you people," she said, as she emerged and began shaking its folds into place. "We mustn't be late."

They made haste, and presently they were out in the flower garden, where most of the Middles were already. Madge Russell, looking at them as they wandered about, sighed to herself. This term's outgoings would be large, and many of her own girls would have left them. The school would go on flourishing, she felt sure. They were firmly established, and she knew that the vacant places were already more than filled, for the fame of the school was spreading. But after this it would not be *her* school as it had been. Perhaps it was as well, for her hands were full as it was, and would probably grow fuller as the years went on. Joey would have only another year at the school, for she was going to Belsornia when she was seventeen, as lady-in-waiting to the princess. Her education would be continued there by masters and governesses with Elisaveta, but she would cease to be a schoolgirl. After that, no one knew what the future held for her. Madge hoped that her writing gifts would bring her something. That was all she would think of at present. She finished her dressing, and went down to join her girls, looking scarcely older than they did, in her dainty white frock and big shady hat. The first guests began to arrive shortly after this, and the afternoon was full and very busy.

Dick and his wife and babies were there, of course, and so were Gisela and her husband. Wanda and Friedel had come from Partenkirchen for two days, so as not to miss this event; and all the old friends were there, as well as some new ones, among whom was Herr von der Witt, highly delighted with everything and everybody.

The girls gave a concert in the garden, and sang some of the lovely old madrigals that Mr Denny revelled in. Margia and Grizel both played, and Frieda enchanted everyone by her lovely harp solo. Joey sang two folk songs, and, of course, they showed some of the folk dances, and Herr von der Witt was actually heard to say that it was a very pretty sight. As his two ideas in life were fresh air and geology, they all felt that this was a great compliment.

Then *Kaffee* was served, the girls acting as waitresses, and after that people began to make a move homewards in the playing fields, the girls clustered together for a last speech from their head girl.

Grizel looked round them all. "You are dears," she began uncertainly. Then she stopped. She felt that if she went on she would break down.

Joey guessed what she was feeling, and sprang into the breech. "Three cheers for Grizel, one of the best head girls the school has ever had!" she yelled at the top of her voice. They were given with a vim that made those of the guests who still remained literally jump, and sent Grizel flying to a place of refuge before she should disgrace herself in front of them all by crying.

Jo found her later, looking rather red about the eyes, but very happy. "Good for you, Grizel!" she said.

Grizel looked round at the lovely lake with the huge mountains towering all round it; the flower garden, quiet now that all the guests were gone; the chalet, where she had spent four happy years; finally at the girl who had stood by her through so much. "It's been a good time, Joey," she said. "All my life I shall remember how much I owe you, and Madame, and the Chalet School."

THE END

The Chalet School
Elinor M. Brent-Dyer

Elinor M. Brent-Dyer has written many books about life at the famous Alpine school. Follow the thrilling adventures of Joey, Mary-Lou and all the other well-loved characters in this delightful series.

Below is a list of Chalet School titles always available in Armada. For details of all available titles in the series, write to:

Armada, HarperCollins Children's Books,
77–85 Fulham Palace Road, Hammersmith,
London W6 8JB

1	The School at the Chalet	£2.99	☐
2	Jo of the Chalet School	£2.99	☐
3	The Princess of the Chalet School	£2.99	☐
4	The Head Girl of the Chalet School	£2.99	☐
5	Rivals of the Chalet School	£2.99	☐
6	Eustacia Goes to the Chalet School	£2.99	☐
7	The Chalet School and Jo	£2.99	☐
8	The Chalet Girls in Camp	£2.99	☐
9	Exploits of the Chalet Girls	£2.99	☐
10	The Chalet School and the Lintons	£2.99	☐
11	A Rebel in the Chalet School	£2.99	☐
12	The New House at the Chalet School	£2.99	☐

All these books are available at your local bookshop or newsagent, or can be ordered from the publisher. To order direct from the publishers just tick the title you want and fill in the form below:

Name _____

Address _____

_____

Send to: HarperCollins Children's Cash Sales
            PO Box 11
            Falmouth
            Cornwall
            TR10 9EN

Please enclose a cheque or postal order or debit my Visa/Access –

            Credit card no:
            Expiry date:
            Signature:

– to the value of the cover price plus:
UK: 60p for the first book, 25p for the second book, plus 15p per copy for each additional book ordered to a maximum charge of £1.90.

BFPO: 60p for the first book, 25p for the second book plus 15p per copy for the next 7 books, thereafter 9p per book.

Overseas and Eire: £1.25 for the first book, 75p for the second book. Thereafter 28p per book.